WHISLING ISLAND NIGHTS

A WHISLING ISLAND NOVEL

JULIA CLEMENS

PICKLED PLUM PUBLISHING

Laura
The best social media manager who isn't really my social media manager a girl could ask for

CHAPTER ONE

"THEY'RE GONE," Amber said, her face pale as she looked up to where Nora was descending the stairs.

"What?" Nora stopped mid-step, her seven am weekend brain trying to wrap itself around what Amber had said. Who were gone? Were they okay? Judging by Amber's look of fear, probably not.

"Dad and Raul. They went to breakfast," Amber said, referring to her adoptive father and fiancé. Her expression was still apprehensive but Nora breathed a sigh of relief.

Thank goodness. No one was in danger.

"Amber, don't scare me like that," she admonished, taking the last of the stairs and sinking down onto the couch of the rental that she, Amber, and Raul had been sharing with Amber's adoptive parents, Gerry and Tabby, along with Amber's sister Elise since the evening before.

They were taking a weekend away, the people most important to Amber, to get to know her fiancé, Raul. A man she'd only begun dating a few weeks before but was now marrying so he wouldn't be deported back to his home country of Argentina.

No, that wasn't fair. According to both Amber and Raul, they were deeply in love and would have married anyway. Raul's pending deportment just pushed the timeline forward.

But Amber's adoptive parents and sister, along with Nora, weren't convinced that this was the whole story. They knew Amber was telling them the truth but they didn't know Raul well enough to be sure of his sincerity. Amber was a successful, beautiful, vibrant, and loving woman. Raul would literally win the wife lottery when he married Amber. And while he doubtless had his winning points as well, he was the one who'd own part of a thriving business if he married Amber. He was the one who wouldn't be deported. Amber's family considered that Raul was getting a really great deal with this marriage, while Amber . . . she'd be putting a lot on the line.

But there was something Nora knew that Gerry, Tabby, and Elise didn't. If this weekend didn't go well, if the family didn't show their support for the wedding at the end of this, Amber was threatening to elope. So Nora, the only one who knew what was truly at stake, was frantically trying to manage all sides without going insane.

She had to keep it together.

Although Amber declaring people were gone in such a terrified manner was doing nothing to help Nora preserve what was left of her ever-diminishing sanity.

"Mama Nora. It's Dad and Raul . . . alone," Amber said, walking from the kitchen to join Nora on the couch. Nora had a moment's regret that she hadn't stayed in bed a little longer. But her worries along with the unfamiliar bed hadn't allowed her a restful night, so after hours of tossing and turning she'd finally called it quits a little before seven and had decided to start loading up on coffee ASAP. Now, however, it looked like that coffee would have to wait. Nora had made the mistake of falling into the couch and its comfortable depths had swallowed her whole. She'd make her way out to coffee soon. But right now she could use a blanket and some snuggles.

Too bad her handsome boyfriend, Mack, was back home.

But this weekend was about Raul and Amber. And while she would have loved to have Mack by her side, that would have encouraged Bobby, Nora's high school boyfriend and Amber's father, to tag along as well and the man was drama. Nora had enough of that on her plate without adding Bobby to the mix. So she'd sacrificed time with Mack this weekend to help her keep her peace of mind and hopefully work things out between Amber and the family.

Right now she was regretting that decision.

"At breakfast," Nora said. She'd waited for Amber to continue her thought but it had stopped after 'alone' so Nora finished it for her, laying a reassuring hand on her daughter's knee. It wasn't as if Gerry and Raul were out hunting or fighting to the death or . . . Nora's brain was too tired to think of any other dangerous activities that a soon-to-be father-in-law would coerce his daughter's fiancé to do with him.

"Yes, breakfast. But that's all I was told. Where are they? Why wasn't I invited? Poor Raul." Amber leaned forward and groaned, dropping her head into her hands.

Nora didn't have patience for these melodramatics, especially before her coffee. But even her tired brain understood that anything other than kind words while Amber was in this state wouldn't work out well for anyone in the end.

"Probably because your dad didn't want you along. It's a very normal thing for a dad to grill his daughter's fiancé," Nora said as she sat up so that her back was no longer enveloped by couch cushions. She was now one step closer to coffee.

"Do you really think that's what he's doing?" Amber asked, her eyes wide with horror.

"Probably. This is a good thing, Amber. This means your

dad is accepting the idea that Raul is who you chose. If he really was intent on you two never marrying—" Nora paused. This was why Amber wanted to elope. She'd feared her family would never accept her choice of a husband. But it was much more complicated than simply liking him. They were all afraid that Raul was using Amber. A valid fear. They also felt Amber should slow down, give herself time to really think through this. Again, a valid concern. But Amber had been so wrapped up in the pain of her family sharing these concerns rather than whole-heartedly supporting her that she'd thought the worst of them.

And because this reaction wasn't typical for Amber, Nora worried that Raul had encouraged these uncharitable thoughts about her family. So on top of all the details the others knew, Nora had her own set of concerns about her daughter's fiancé. She dragged her thoughts back to the present as Amber's raised eyebrows reminded her she'd stopped in the middle of her sentence. "Your dad wouldn't be taking this time with him."

Amber cocked her head to the side as she considered Nora's words. Nora, suddenly a bit more awake, capitalized on her burst of energy and pushed herself off of the couch, propelling herself toward the kitchen and the Keurig on the counter.

"You might be right," Amber conceded as she considered Nora's words.

Nora, her attention on the coffee machine, said, "I'm probably not wrong."

Okay, not her best work. She needed caffeine.

Amber glanced up at her birth mom and Nora shrugged before pointing at the coffee pot.

"Right." Amber gave a little smile of understanding.

Neither woman functioned very well without their morning cup of Joe. So Amber must have already consumed hers.

Nora put a pod in the machine and filled it with water before grabbing a mug to place under the spigot. Glancing toward the sink, she spotted a used mug waiting to be washed. Yup, Amber was indeed one step ahead of Nora.

"Should I try to find them?" Amber asked just as Nora's mug finished filling.

Nora didn't say a word. She needed to be fortified before she answered that question. She had a feeling that her instinctive response of *no, you idiot* wouldn't go over well.

"They probably wouldn't have gone into the city just for breakfast, right?" Amber rambled on even though Nora hadn't responded.

And Amber was probably right. The cute rental they'd gotten for the weekend, right on the beach, was a little outside of Seattle's downtown. It was close enough to drive into the city for the day, but there were many closer eateries that Nora was sure Gerry and Raul would have chosen.

But again, coffee had yet to touch her lips. Nora was holding her peace until that happened.

Brewing finally complete, Nora added a touch of creamer and lifted the mug to her face, taking a moment to bask in the aroma before taking a sip. What she really wanted to do was gulp the thing down, but that would literally burn her from the inside out. So she settled for that sip, savoring it before finally speaking.

"Yes, they probably stayed close. But no, don't look for them, Amber. If they'd wanted you there they would have invited you." Nora took a second sip and then a third, moving the caffeine from the mug to her body as quickly as possible.

"Maybe Dad ambushed Raul," Amber speculated as she crossed her arms over her chest and looked out through the sliding glass door to the seashore just steps away.

"Or maybe they were both up early and your dad decided to treat his future son-in-law to a nice breakfast," Nora countered.

Amber shook her head. "That doesn't sound at all like Dad.

He has to wake up early for work in his day-to-day life so he always sleeps in on vacations. Something is up, Mama Nora." Amber pursed her lips.

Nora sighed softly, too softly for Amber to hear. There was a chance Amber was right. But if this was what Gerry needed to do to feel good about this union, why would Amber begrudge her father the chance for peace of mind? It worried Nora that the only person Amber seemed concerned about in this situation was Raul. Nora wished Amber would take a second to think about someone else—especially herself.

"Amber, if you want your family to accept Raul, you are going to need to let things like this happen," Nora said as she rounded the kitchen counter and joined Amber in the living room.

She was about to return to the too-comfortable couch when Amber shook her head and pointed toward the back door.

Nora nodded, understanding that Amber wanted to speak with her outside.

The two made their way toward the door, Nora with her mug—she wasn't about to leave that behind—and Amber slid the door open. The chilly morning air coming off of the ocean hit them immediately.

With one wordless, shared look both women turned back to grab their coats from the front closet before heading out into the near-frigid air. Because it was September, the days were mostly mild but right on the ocean like this, the mornings could be downright chilly.

Amber closed the sliding door behind them and headed toward the shore. Nora followed, keeping up step for step.

"Do you really think that this is my family trying?" Amber asked as she stopped abruptly, turning to face Nora.

Nora stepped close to her daughter. "That is definitely what I see. Isn't that what you see?"

Amber shrugged. "It's what I'm hoping for. But because I want it so badly I'm worried I'll see it even if that's not what's actually happening."

Nora's heart hurt for her daughter. She was having the internal battle of a lifetime and needed her mother's help. But Nora also knew she needed to be careful with her words. Anything said the wrong way could tip the scales. One misstep, and everything could go downhill. Amber would end up marrying the wrong man without her family present.

That wasn't fair. Nora wasn't completely convinced that Raul was the wrong man for Amber. He'd been charming in the time they'd spent together, attentive of Amber. Nora's main concern was the influence he seemed to have over his fiancée. The fact that she'd even considered an elopement was completely out of character. Nora suspected Raul was the one pushing for that, as well as causing Amber's negative outlook on her family's actions.

But maybe it wasn't the case. Nora was trying to give Raul the benefit of the doubt, for all of their sakes.

"Amber, your family loves you. Everything they do, right or wrong in your eyes, they are doing because of that love. Maybe it isn't what you want, and maybe it's not even what's best for you, but it is their best. Because they have and will always give you their very best," Nora said honestly. She hadn't known Amber's adoptive family for very long but in even that short time she knew this to be true.

She watched as Amber turned toward the gray ocean and shuffled a foot back and forth, her internal conflict clear on her face. The ground below them was more rocky than actual grains of sand—a mixture of browns, grays, whites, and blacks. The sun was just beginning to fully show itself above the horizon and the light spilling across the water created a perfect picture. Other than the scowl marring Amber's gorgeous face.

"That's the thing though. If they're really trying their hardest, how can they not even give Raul a chance?" Amber asked, still glaring at the sunrise.

Nora shook her head. "I don't think that's exactly fair to them, Amber. They are here. For the sole purpose of getting to know Raul. Your dad is out to breakfast with him."

Amber opened her mouth but Nora raised her hand.

"I get it. The breakfast might be a grilling of more than just bacon and sausages, but your dad is putting time into a relationship he wouldn't care to cultivate were it not for you," Nora continued.

Amber bit her lip and finally gave a single nod.

Thank goodness. They were finally getting somewhere.

"And your mom stayed up past midnight to play games with everyone last night. Didn't you say the last time that happened was about four decades ago?" Nora couldn't help but add.

Amber nodded again, less reluctantly this time.

"And Elise hasn't made a single snide remark. In fact, none of them have asked if we could postpone the wedding again," Amber rode on Nora's roll.

This time Nora nodded, trying not to look too eager.

"Are they perfect?" Nora asked before answering the question for herself. "None of us are. Do they probably have their own agenda?"

Amber nodded emphatically.

"But you do too," Nora pointed out gently.

Amber gave a slight frown but didn't disagree.

"What would you do if this were Elise?" Nora asked Amber.

"I would trust her judgment and support her one hundred percent," Amber said without hesitation.

"But you don't know that," Nora said.

Amber rolled her eyes. "I can't *know* anything until I live it."

"How do you think Elise would have answered that question had she been asked it before Raul?" Nora asked.

Amber played with a stray thread on the bottom of her jacket. "The same way I did."

Amber knew her sister well.

"So don't you think you should try to see her side? She's hating that she can't support you completely. She's said that. But there has to be a reason she doesn't. Maybe the reason is valid, or maybe it's not, but don't cut them out of your life."

Nora watched Amber swallow. "I wouldn't be cutting them out of my life . . . " Amber began but paused. She couldn't ignore how much an elopement would strain her relationship with her family. Especially if Amber only invited Nora.

"Give them a chance. If at the end of this weekend they still don't want to see you married, you do you. That's what you have to do. But don't elope. That's taking the choice from your family. Maybe they'll decide on their own that they can't go to the wedding because they don't support it—"

"And that would kill me," Amber interrupted with a whisper.

Oh. Nora finally understood. The elopement wasn't just about marrying Raul with no opposition, it was about pushing her family away before they could reject her.

Now Nora wasn't sure what to say. She wanted to assure Amber that of course her family would be at her wedding no matter what. That they wouldn't stay away just because they felt Amber was making a mistake. But Nora didn't know that for sure. She knew she could answer for herself—even if she was convinced Amber shouldn't marry Raul she would be there. But would Amber's family feel the same? Nora hoped so and she was more than ninety percent sure they would, but that last tiny percentage kept her silent.

"I've dealt with a lot of self-esteem issues over the years. It took me a long time to see that I wasn't abandoned by you but I was chosen by my parents," Amber said, her eyes focused on a wave that was making its way to shore.

Nora put an arm around Amber's shoulders, unable to help herself. How she wished Amber had always known how very wanted and loved she'd been. It was only Nora's immense and all-consuming love for her daughter that had helped her to finally make that heart-wrenching decision to let someone else raise her flesh and blood. Her baby girl. But Nora could see how Amber, without knowing any of that, would have felt deserted. Abandoned. Even though it had been the very opposite: Nora had sacrificed her own chance at raising and loving this beautiful child to give Amber a chance. A chance to be loved by a mother and a father. A chance to be in a house full of love, never wondering when or where the next meal would be. If Nora had kept Amber she couldn't have promised any of that. Not as a seventeen-year-old semi-recovered addict.

"I know that's not the case now," Amber said, her thoughts thankfully along the same lines as Nora's. Nora had told her daughter how wanted she'd been many times and she was glad that message had been received. "But back then it was hard to see it any other way."

Amber wrapped her arms around herself as Nora still held her. Nora hoped the double hug helped.

"I think it's because of my past that I have a hard time dealing with anyone not choosing me. It's why I've hardly had any serious relationships. The second I see even the tiniest of doubts in the other person, I leave first. It's the same thing with my family now. It will hurt like nothing else to have the most special day of my life without them by my side. But the only thing that would hurt worse? For them to choose not to be there. I don't think I can take that chance," Amber whispered the last word as she turned and lifted her eyes to meet Nora's.

Nora hugged Amber closer. What did one say to that? Especially when Nora knew she was the one to have first hurt Amber, even if all she'd done was for Amber's sake.

She noticed tears hitting Amber's cheeks and reached out to gently wipe them away. Why did this have to be so hard?

In a sudden flash of insight, Nora realized just why Raul was so appealing to Amber. Unlike past men, Raul didn't just want Amber. He needed her. Without her he would be deported. He couldn't abandon her, not without losing his precious residency.

Did Amber even really love Raul?

Nora began to suspect Amber had only convinced herself that she did. Her fears ruled and she clung to the person who wouldn't be able to leave her. If Nora pointed out the truth, would Amber see it? Would she have the tools to sift through what she was feeling and pinpoint why she was so adamant about marrying a man she still had so much to learn about?

But now didn't feel like the time to bring this up. Not when Amber was already so vulnerable.

"We would never do that to you."

Nora and Amber both jumped at the sound of a voice behind them.

They turned back to see that sometime during their talk Elise had sneaked up on them. Between the sound of the wind and the cover of trees that dotted the yard behind them it wasn't surprising she'd been able to move so stealthily. But how much had she heard? And was it bad that Nora was grateful she no longer had to carry this burden alone?

"I came out to ask if you both wanted Mom to make you some pancakes but then saw your posture, Amber, and knew you guys were talking about something important. I should apologize for eavesdropping. But I'm not sorry. Especially after what I heard. Were you seriously planning on eloping? Getting married without us?" Elise asked as she stood just in front of Amber, demanding her sister look her in the eyes.

"Elise, I can explain," Amber began, fear flickering through her eyes.

Nora didn't blame her. Her heart was still racing from the scare, but she didn't think Amber had to worry about Elise being mad unless she actually eloped.

"No, don't explain. Because I don't care. All I care about is that it won't happen. Promise me that no matter what I say or do, I won't lose the chance to stand beside the person who means the most to me in this world as she says her vows to the man she chooses." Elise took Amber's hands and squeezed tightly.

"You'd be there even though you hate Raul?" Amber choked, tears now flowing down her face and splashing onto the rocks below.

"I don't hate him, Am. I'm not a fan of you and him together, at least at this moment, but I don't hate him. And even if I did, I would be there. So don't rob me of that, please," Elise begged.

Amber nodded immediately.

"Mom and Dad would feel the same way," Elise continued urgently.

"Are you sure?" Amber asked, her voice tiny against the wind and the crashing surf.

"Absolutely. Because not showing up would be quitting. And you know we never quit on each other," Elise insisted.

Amber nodded as her lips wobbled.

"We will always be there. Always," Elise promised as she tugged on Amber's hands, pulling her into a hug.

Amber melted into her sister.

Nora smiled, her eyes filled with unshed tears. All would be well. Maybe Raul was the wrong guy; maybe he wasn't. But right then none of that mattered as much as Amber knowing her family would be there for her. All of them would be there for her. Always.

CHAPTER TWO

"FANCY SEEING YOU HERE," Piper said, playfully bumping Nora with her hip. She'd come into the grocery store to grab a few items she needed for dinner that evening: two limes, tortilla strips, and extra large tortillas. The sweet pork was bubbling away in her crockpot and the rest of the ingredients were already in her pantry or fridge.

"Oh hey, Pipe," Nora said, holding up the giant fountain drink in her hand. "Just grabbing fortifications for my meeting."

Piper grinned at the cup the size of her head. "Deb holding one for all of her sales team?" she assumed. Nora worked at the island's popular art gallery, owned by one of Whisling's own local talents who happened to be Nora's sister, Deb Johnson.

Nora shook her head. "At the hospital. The volunteers in the—" Nora paused and Piper knew exactly why. Nora had been about to mention the teen hangout at the hospital where she volunteered, where she'd met Piper's daughter Kristie. The hangout was incredible, a place where teens who were struggling with cancer, chemo, and all that life had thrown at them gathered to have fun and just be teens. Where Kristie had often spent time with her boyfriend and had been able to laugh as well as cry. A place Kristie had felt safe even though it was the same place she'd experienced some of her worst moments during treatment. The very same place where Kristie had gotten her terminal diagnosis . . . somehow the teen hangout had made even that news bearable, at least for Kristie.

Suddenly Piper felt tears prick her eyes. Grief was a beast like that. One moment she could be walking into the store for limes and the next she'd be falling apart, her world feeling off kilter forever because her baby girl was gone.

"I'm sorry," Nora said and Piper shook her head. She was hurting but the sorrow wasn't what it had once been. It was like living with chronic pain; it would always be there but Piper had to learn to function with it. So she did. And she didn't need people to accommodate conversations for her. At least not anymore.

"I'm okay. I just had a moment."

"I get it." Nora set down her cup to give Piper a hug, which Piper gladly returned. No matter that they were in the middle of the grocery store.

People walked past, some giving Piper and Nora strange looks but most commiserating with them. That was one of the benefits of living on a small island. Most knew what Piper had endured.

"I didn't realize you still volunteer," Piper said as she pulled out of the hug and gathered herself. "I mean, it makes sense that you do, but it's just hard to remember that those parts of the world still go on . . . "

Piper didn't need to finish with *after Kristie left this life.*

"Yeah. Not as often as I'd like to. But I try to go every other week or so."

Piper nodded. Nora was amazing like that. She went in and was what those kids needed, allowing her heart to get attached even while knowing it would eventually be broken. The odds weren't good for any of them.

"And Mack goes too?" Piper asked.

Nora nodded. "He's waiting for me in the car."

"Then I should let you go," Piper said, stepping to the side so Nora could make her way to the registers.

Nora paused, her head tilting as she considered Piper.

"Please feel free to say no," she began cautiously.

Piper wasn't sure what was coming next but she held her breath as she nodded once.

"We're actually meeting as a big group. Some of us volunteers, a few parents, and then our fundraising committee."

"I didn't know you all were so organized," Piper replied, not feeling quite the trepidation she had been.

"We weren't. Until recently. Have you met Seren Lamb?" Nora asked.

Piper shook her head, unable to recall the name.

"You two actually have quite a bit in common," Nora said and Piper instantly knew what that meant. Seren had lost a child as well.

"How long ago?" Piper asked in a low voice. She wasn't sure why but she wanted to know.

"Three years now. She has quite the story, but I'll let her tell you herself one day. Anyway, she's a transplant to the island. Moved here—"

"About three years ago." Piper knew the answer without knowing the woman. When you lose a child nothing feels right. You make big changes, new decisions, shake things up just to see if you can feel again. Piper had considered moving, making a fresh start, but she couldn't leave Kristie behind.

Nora nodded. "She's kept to herself for most of that time."

Piper didn't blame her.

"But she came to the hospital about a month ago, asking how

she could help our specific cause. She did a walk of our teen room and deemed it inadequate. It's something Mack and I have been thinking for a while but weren't sure what to do. Seren's taken charge and now we're fundraising to fix up a cottage on the back of hospital property. Seren somehow managed to convince the administration that an updated teen hangout would be the best use for the building and we are rocking and rolling."

"She sounds like a force," Piper said, feeling exhausted just listening to Nora.

"She is. I think you'd like her."

Piper didn't doubt it.

"So would you like to meet her? Come to the meeting with me?"

Oh. Piper should have seen the invitation coming but was still surprised by it. It made sense for her to go. If anyone in the community had profited from the teen hangout and their volunteers, it had been Kristie, and Piper by extension. But she'd avoided everything to do with the hospital since Kristie's death. She just couldn't manage it.

Even though she knew refusing would make Kristie sad. Although the hospital had held so much hardship for Kristie, it was also a pivotal place in her childhood, cruel though it may be, and she wouldn't have wanted Piper to avoid a place that was so meaningful to her. For every painful moment that the hospital had had for Kristie, it also held a bright spot, whether it be a nurse Kristie had loved or Nora or her friends at the teen hangout.

Piper owed that hospital so much. But could she go back?

"The hospital . . . " Piper began and Nora quickly shook her head.

"The meeting is at Seren's home on the hillside," Nora explained. "I wouldn't ask you to go back to the hospital."

Piper let out a breath of relief.

Maybe she could do this. She had been looking for more ways to serve, put herself out there. And this would be ideal. She could help the hospital without going there, support the kids who had been there for Kristie without hanging out with them. It wasn't that Piper wanted to avoid those sweet kids; she just didn't know how to interact with them now that . . .

But this . . . this seemed possible. Even plausible.

She'd been taking slow but sure steps forward in the past few months, beginning to see the silver lining, and even catching glimpses of how life could one day be bright again. But she knew there would be so many struggles ahead. Maybe this would be a way to find some purpose on those days when she felt nothing.

"You don't have to commit to anything," Nora promised and that sealed the deal.

"Lead the way." Piper motioned forward and Nora grinned.

They paid for their items before heading for their respective cars, Mack waving when he saw Piper exiting the store with Nora.

She then followed Mack's car. They drove toward the hillside where many of the nicest homes on the island had been built, including the mansion belonging to movie star and Piper's friend Julia, as well as Julia's country music star boyfriend's house. It made Piper even more curious about Seren.

Mack stopped at a gate before pressing a button on an intercom.

Oh shoot. Did they need to be buzzed in? Piper had no idea what she'd say. *I'm here with Nora?*

But she didn't have to worry. The gate swung open and Mack waved for Piper to follow him up a small hill to a circular driveway. Piper took in the house attached to said driveway, which was at least four times the size of Piper's own.

Piper parked her car and remained in her seat, gawking at the house. She knew it wasn't polite but in her own car couldn't she do as she wanted?

Nora knocked on Piper's window.

Piper opened her door.

"Not quite what you were expecting?" Nora asked, her eyes following Piper's gaze to the natural white stone that made up the exterior of the entire home. Black window panes broke up the stark white outside, along with vibrant green vegetation lining the ground level. But Piper only noticed these in her peripheral vision, as she couldn't drag her eyes away from the wraparound porch of her dreams. It was just so pretty.

"You could have warned me Seren has money," Piper said with raised eyebrows.

"And ruined the surprise? Besides, once you meet her you'll see that she's nothing like her house," Nora said.

Piper wasn't sure what that meant. But Nora was walking to the house now, so she hurried to gather her things and catch up.

Piper's ratty tennis shoes and her going-to-get-groceries leggings now made her feel sorely underdressed. Thankfully Nora was in jeans and a t-shirt so Piper didn't feel too out of place, but what would Seren think? Piper's first impression was going to be less than stellar.

"Nora!" A high-pitched squeal escaped the house as the black front door was flung open.

If Piper had felt underdressed, she now actually kind of felt overdressed as she took in Seren's appearance. The woman was undoubtedly beautiful with her waist-length raven locks and hazel eyes. But it was her outfit and tiny stature that stunned Piper. Seren couldn't be taller than five feet and in her sweats and band T she looked just a few years older than Kristie, not like a mother who'd lost a child.

But as Piper took a closer look she saw that Seren's tennis

shoes cost more than what Piper charged for an entire photography session and the sweats and band T looked like they were custom made for her. Even though Seren was casual, her outfit was probably still worth nearly the same amount as Piper's reliable but old car.

Piper was finding that Nora was probably right in her assessment earlier. She might already like Seren and they hadn't even exchanged a word. She was at least intrigued.

"How was the weekend?" Seren asked Nora immediately, making Piper feel like the worst friend ever. She'd forgotten about Nora's trip to Seattle with her daughter and her family, as well as Amber's fiancé.

"Better than I expected," Nora said as she pulled out of Seren's hug. "But there's still a lot to do."

Seren nodded as if she understood. She probably did since she remembered to ask about things and Piper evidently just thought about herself.

"I'm sorry I didn't ask earlier," Piper said to Nora who immediately shook her head.

"Don't you worry. I railroaded our earlier conversation. You were hardly able to get a word in. You didn't have a chance, especially with what I was throwing at you," Nora said kindly, even though that hadn't been the case at all.

"And I see your beautiful man locking up your car, but who, gorgeous, are you?" Seren asked, turning to Piper with a welcoming smile.

"This is Piper—" Nora didn't get a chance to finish the introduction as Seren pounced, hugging Piper and speaking all at once.

"I have heard all about you!" Seren said excitedly. "I'm sure we'll be fast friends. I know people assume all kinds of things about moms who've lost, but in this case, I just feel in my gut they were right. Don't you?"

Some might say Seren was like a whirlwind but Piper found her to be a breath of fresh air.

"I do," Piper said honestly.

Seren kept an arm around Piper's shoulders as she led her into her home.

"Bring that yummy man and you all come on in. Most of the others are already here," Seren called back to Nora.

Piper wasn't sure what to think. Seren dressed like a teenager and yet she spoke like an eighty-year-old. The more Piper got to know Seren the more she wanted to know.

"Now I'm sure Nora brought you here saying you wouldn't have to commit. People tend to baby us, don't you think?" Seren asked but before Piper could respond she pressed on. "I'm not going to baby you. I see you: a woman with two hands, a sound mind, and a gorgeous face. Let's put all that to work. I need someone to help me head up this fundraising effort. I have a ton of contacts who love to throw their money at all kinds of stupid causes, but it's hard to get them to focus. You, gorgeous, you'll get them to focus and then I'll come in and scoop all that money right up."

Piper felt her mouth drop open. What was happening? Yet despite her confusion, she found herself kind of enjoying it.

"I know it sounds terrible. And if we were getting the money for anything other than our worthy cause, I'd feel horrible. But those teens need something better. We're going to get it for them. And yet our cause doesn't have the glitz and glam of a diamond-crusted iguana exhibit or a new rehab facility on the moon."

Were those real things or was Seren making them up? They sounded fake. They should be fake, but with Seren it felt like anything was possible.

"We have to get them to focus on us. I've got the silver

tongue but you've got the golden face. With the two of us teamed up, the world won't know what hit 'em."

Seren pumped her eyebrows and Piper found herself nodding even though she hardly had an idea of what she was truly signing up for.

"Good. So you'll co-lead this fundraising effort with me. Now that that's settled, let's introduce you to everyone else."

And that was how Piper found herself at the head of a fundraising effort she hadn't known about even an hour before. Thankfully she believed in the cause.

"DID SHE REALLY SAY 'GOLDEN FACE'?" Carter asked, his eyes filled with mirth.

Piper didn't blame him. She'd spent more time laughing than actually being able to recount her afternoon.

Even though Carter was technically her ex-husband, he was over for dinner, having Piper's favorite copycat TexMex salad. The same way he'd been over for dinner every night for the past month or more, ever since they'd decided to explore whatever this was between them.

For now, they were exes who got along a little too well and loved spending time together. Friends on the verge of . . .

Piper knew if she recounted her story to others they wouldn't understand how Carter could be back in her life. He'd left her and Kristie.

But it had been a foolish young adult mistake that he'd spent these past few years trying to atone for, the worst and best years of Piper's life. During that time Carter had been her rock when he hadn't had to be. He had been there for Kristie, loved her hard, never allowed her to doubt anything, and had done the same for Piper.

So yeah, Carter was back. Not only because he wanted to be. Piper wanted him as well.

But the state of their relationship was confusing as heck.

"I kind of love it," Carter said as he considered the term.

"Me too!" Piper exclaimed. It was the weirdest yet one of the best compliments she'd ever received.

"I think I get what she means," Carter continued.

"Right?" Piper agreed.

Was that conceited to agree? No, she was just accepting a compliment. An area she was trying to improve.

"So she's a rich lady. You aren't sure how young or old she is," Carter said as he took a bite of his salad.

Piper dug into her own. It had been neglected as she'd rambled on and on about her afternoon and Carter had sat there listening, enjoying every moment of it.

When things were good with Carter, life was better than she could imagine. And even though Piper had forgiven Carter for leaving, a tiny part of her was still scared. She knew he didn't leave when times got rough, but what if life got boring again? Would he want to stay then? Because the only thing worse than Carter leaving again would be if he stayed just because he'd said he would. If Carter wanted to fly, Piper wanted to see him soar. She would not be the reason he was stuck groundside.

But now wasn't the time to worry about that. She and Carter were just living. Enjoying life. Seeing what was there. Exploring. Maybe letting things get a little boring to see what Carter would do. And so far Piper's life was about as unexciting as it could possibly be, Seren aside, and Carter was still there.

Hm.

Wait, she wasn't worrying about it. Right.

They were talking about Seren.

"I'm pretty sure she's close to our age," Piper said. If she had to guess that's where her estimate would land. But she could be way off.

"Does she have any other kids?" Carter was now on the case. Seren was too intriguing for them to leave alone. She had a backstory and, like Piper, Carter wanted to know it.

"Just the one she lost, as far as I know."

"How old was the child?" Carter asked softly, his eyes filled with the understanding and pain that only a man who'd also endured such a loss could have.

"Too young," Piper said as she tried to swallow down the lettuce that wouldn't dislodge now that her throat was so dry. All of those kids were too young, but Seren's appeared younger than most from the photos Piper had seen in her home. "The picture where he looks the oldest is probably around seven or eight?"

Carter's Adam's apple bobbed.

Piper nodded as she was finally able to swallow.

They got it.

Without a word, they got it.

"A husband?" Carter asked.

"Why? Are you interested in the position?" Piper asked, her head tilting mischievously before she popped in another forkful of salad.

"For Seren? Absolutely not. But for you?"

Piper held her breath, her mouthful of salad forgotten.

"Is the position open?" Carter asked.

Was the position open? What kind of question was that? Carter had once had it and then thrown it away. No, she wasn't going back there. Piper was beyond this. But—but . . . Piper was just grateful her sputtering was only in her mind.

"I'm not sure," she finally answered honestly, speaking around her food because she hadn't been able to chew and nearly lose her mind at the same time.

Carter pulled off a piece of tortilla and popped it into his mouth. "For the record, I'm interested. But I'm not pushing. I'm willing to wait as long as you need me to."

He was interested. In taking the role of Piper's husband. What?! She'd thought it might be a possibility; Carter had hinted at wanting more and if they'd been married once it kinda made sense, but to hear it aloud . . . Why wasn't he pushing? But she didn't want him to push, did she?

She was a mess. A confused, excited mess.

"There was a guy in the pictures, but she didn't talk about him." Piper finally managed to answer Carter's earlier question. The rest had her thoughts and emotions in a jumble and she'd deal with it later. Or she wouldn't. That was more her M.O. as of late.

"Intriguing," Carter said as he dipped another piece of tortilla into his dressing.

"I thought so too," Piper replied, regaining her ability to breathe normally, thanks to the change of topic.

"Do you know why she moved to Whisling?" Carter asked.

Piper shook her head. "But I do know her son is buried here. In the same cemetery as Kristie." Piper's voice broke on the word *cemetery*. A word she should have never had to say in the same sentence as her daughter's name. Losing a child went against nature. It was just that wrong.

Carter pushed out of his chair and made his way around the table. As he knelt next to Piper he was still almost her same height. Wordlessly he pulled her into his arms.

Carter had done this almost every day. Simply held Piper in the moments she'd needed it. He never asked for anything in return, and it never turned to more. It was just a hug of comfort when Piper needed it most.

She let herself relish the feeling of safety she could only find in Carter's arms. She'd been held countless times in the past few months, by her mom, dad, friends, and strangers. Yet only Carter's embrace gave her the sense of belonging. Of being. She was only truly Piper when she was being held by Carter.

So as confusing as her thoughts and emotions were regarding Carter, she would have to deal with them someday. She'd have to figure out what she felt. Because if she couldn't give Carter anything in return, no matter how much he said he would wait forever for her, Piper would have to let him go.

And short of losing Kristie, nothing scared her more.

But for Carter she would do it.

CHAPTER THREE

EMMA STRUMMED the last chord of the simple song as Jax, their guitar instructor, clapped.

"You practiced a lot, didn't you?" Jax asked in his sexy Australian accent, a proud smile on his face showcasing his perfectly placed dimple.

Emma, all of a sudden shy, nodded in response but her smile matched Jax's.

"I can tell," Jax continued to praise.

Lou reveled in the moment as she watched the exchange between her daughter and their teacher. The man had moved to Whisling recently after a career as a guitar and bass player for some of the biggest names in the music industry. Despite his success, at the ripe old age of twenty-nine Jax had decided he'd had enough of that world and wanted to slow down. So he came to Whisling to teach guitar to the rich and sometimes famous who'd made Whisling their home—or second or even third home. Oh, and to Emma and Lou as well.

When Emma had heard of the opportunity for guitar lessons she'd begged for the chance to take them. But when Lou heard Jax's guitar pedigree she knew there was no way she'd be able to afford lessons from him. She'd been complaining to her dad about it at work one day when he mentioned that Jax had just been in to the gym they owned earlier that day, inquiring about a membership. He suggested that maybe Lou could work something out with Jax. So she had. In exchange for a free gym membership, Lou and Emma got discounted lessons twice a month. And Lou became mom of the year in Emma's book, so it had worked out well for all. Especially Lou. Who not only got to take lessons from the hot new guy on the island but also frequently ran into him at the gym . . . shirtless.

"Did your mom practice as much as you did?" Jax asked Emma.

Emma shook her head, unashamedly ratting her mother out.

"Hey," Lou protested, even though she didn't have a leg to stand on. Emma was right. Lou hadn't practiced nearly as much as Emma had or even as much as she should have. Where Emma had mastered the simple chords they'd begun to learn, Lou still messed up more often than she got them right.

"You disagree?" Jax asked, turning his green eyes to her.

Holy moly, the man had a smolder.

Lou quickly shook her head. She couldn't lie to that smolder.

Jax grinned as he leaned back into the couch in the music studio where he gave lessons. Emma and Lou sat on stools facing him, a guitar propped in each of their laps. Not only had Jax agreed to the discounted lessons, but he'd even allowed Lou to borrow one of his guitars when they came for lessons so that she wouldn't have to buy another one. The one Emma now held had set Lou back enough pennies.

Behind Lou and Emma was a digital audio workstation and other mechanics for recording that Lou didn't understand, and beyond that was a window that allowed a peek into the room with microphones set up where Jax did his actual recording.

When Emma had first walked into the recording/lessons space she'd had actual stars in her eyes. Lou hadn't known music had been her oldest daughter's ambition until these lessons and it had been beautiful to see her little girl develop her talents. Not only was Emma determined to learn the guitar, but she had now started writing her own little tunes and Lou couldn't be prouder.

"Okay, Lou, let's see what you've got," Jax said, crossing his muscular arms over his chest. Had Lou mentioned Jax spent a lot of time in the gym?

Lou looked down at her guitar, determined to ignore the charming man sitting just across from her. He was only paying her any attention because she was literally paying him to notice her. Okay, not exactly notice her, but she was paying for lessons and . . . Lou cleared her throat and ducked her head a little farther. So much for ignoring the man; she was only managing to ignore her lesson.

Lou pressed her fingers against the strings at the neck of the guitar, the strong metal digging into the soft flesh of her fingertips. Unlike Emma who was already developing the calluses all good guitar players had, Lou hadn't practiced nearly enough to gain them. It still hurt every time she had to play.

She then strummed with the pick that she still used—Emma had graduated to strumming with her fingers—and the sound that came from the guitar wasn't anywhere near right.

Emma stifled a giggle as Jax bit his lip. Lou felt her face flame red. Sure, she hadn't practiced a ton, but she'd expected to at least get the first chord right.

"I can do that better," Lou promised as she held the guitar even tighter and strummed yet again.

This time the sound that came from her guitar was somehow worse.

Poor Emma couldn't help but cringe.

Same, Emma. Same, Lou thought, avoiding eye contact with Jax.

Jax stood and Lou knew she was in trouble. It didn't matter that she was a grown adult of twenty-eight years and was taking these lessons for fun. She felt like she was back in middle school and had failed a test.

Jax took the few steps between them and placed his hands over Lou's.

"Relax," he said calmly as he tried to loosen Lou's death grip on his guitar.

Didn't he know that this was only making things worse? Nothing could have made Lou more tense than Jax's hands on hers.

Even as Lou told her brain to do as Jax had said, her body just curled right up on itself, an SOS warning sounding in her brain that if she didn't get some space between herself and her teacher, she would spontaneously combust.

Jax finally released her hands and Lou's limbs felt like spaghetti. Was that loose enough?

She tentatively tried the chord again and it finally sounded right.

Hallelujah!

Now to get through the rest of the song.

And although it wasn't perfect—heck, it wasn't even pretty—Lou made it through, thanks to the one instruction Jax had given. He really was an amazing teacher.

"Nice, Lou," Jax said. His voice carried much less enthusiasm than when he'd praised Emma, but Lou felt grateful even for that. She'd done just north of terribly.

"So, Emma," Jax turned his attention to his better student and Lou breathed a sigh of relief. Maybe she should just let Emma take these lessons on her own. This was Emma's passion, after all.

But when Jax had offered them both the discounted lessons Lou had hoped this would be a wonderful opportunity for mother and daughter to spend some time together doing something Emma loved. Emma had been delighted by the idea, so it was a done deal.

Ever since Lou's talk with Deb a few months back, she had worked hard to focus on her relationships with her children. She'd finally gotten it through her thick head that she could not control a single thing her ex, Harvey, did. Whether he left Lou so he could live with a new woman or even when it came to the amount of time he spent with his kids—it wasn't up to Lou.

But what Lou could control was what she did for her kids. So the things that she'd expected Harvey to do, the ways she hoped he'd step up, Lou stepped up instead. From taking these lessons with Emma to coaching Cash's soccer team. She'd even started teaching some of the dance classes at the gym once again. That last one had been harder for Lou to do. It felt selfish, but she realized that caring for herself, taking time to improve herself in the ways she cared about, made her much happier and way less bitter toward Harvey. The fact that she'd lost a good amount of the weight she'd put on during the aftermath of her marriage's demise was just gravy.

"You can keep working on that song while I help Emma with her new stuff." Jax's voice as he turned back to look at Lou brought her out of her thoughts.

"Right," Lou said as if she'd just been waiting for permission to play, not contemplating quitting.

She gently pressed her fingers to the strings and strummed once more.

Lou bit her lip. She really was so bad at this.

But when Lou looked up she saw Emma craning her neck to look beyond Jax, an encouraging smile on her daughter's lips.

Emma believed in her. Lou had noticed the recent change in the way all of her children treated her, especially Emma.

Because unlike the others, Emma hadn't been oblivious to the hurt Harvey had caused Lou. The younger children had been too caught up in Harvey's habit of making them promises and then breaking them. Emma felt all of that hurt as well, but she was able to look beyond that to see her mother's suffering.

So no one had been happier than Emma when Lou had picked herself up and decided she was ready to leave Harvey behind. Not that Emma didn't love her dad—that relationship was so complicated Lou didn't like thinking about it—but when Emma saw that her mom was moving on, it was as if that gave Emma permission to do the same. To push beyond the pain her father had inflicted on her heart and enjoy her life despite all of that.

Lou smiled back at her daughter and then concentrated on her guitar. She couldn't quit. Not when Emma looked at her like that.

Slowly, as Lou played, things sounded a little less wrong. Not quite right, but hey, she was improving. And if she could find time in her schedule to actually practice she might finally get the song right. But between coaching, teaching classes, her job at the gym, being a mom, and then giving herself a few moments to be a woman, Lou wasn't quite sure where practice time would fit in.

But for Emma's sake she'd find it.

"Think you've got it?" Jax asked Emma, causing Lou to look up. According to the clock behind the couch she'd been practicing for twenty minutes straight. Longer than Lou had ever been able to practice in one chunk before. And the song was definitely improving. Who would have thought?

Emma nodded and Jax displayed that dimple once more.

"I expect you to be able to play it by our next lesson," Jax said with confidence.

Emma immediately nodded again and Lou knew Emma wouldn't let him down. That was Lou's job.

Emma stood and Lou followed suit. Their lesson time was up and it wasn't like Jax needed to give Lou a new assignment since she hadn't mastered her last song.

"Where do you think you're going?" Jax turned to Lou, his dimple deepening, laughter in his voice.

Lou loved how laid back Jax was about everything. For Lou, living sometimes felt like an assignment, a task list she had to force herself to complete, whereas it seemed for Jax each morning was a new adventure for him to use as he liked. And since Lou had four kids while Jax was free as a bird, her assessment wasn't far off. Not that Lou didn't love her life; she truly did. She wouldn't trade her kids for the world, but she couldn't help feeling a little envious of Jax's freedom. Lou knew she'd have it someday, when her youngest Hazel left her nest, and she'd probably hate it then, but for now maybe she could ask Jax a few questions about his life and live a bit of that freedom vicariously.

"Time's up," Lou said as she pointed to the clock.

"I don't mind a few more minutes of lessons if you two don't have anywhere to be," Jax said.

Surprisingly, Lou didn't, thanks to her angel of a stepmom. Margie took Lou's younger three during every guitar lesson. And today not only was she taking them for the half hour lesson, but she'd offered to keep the kids until Cash's soccer game that started about an hour after lessons, since Margie and Lou's dad, Bill, would be attending the game anyway.

Lou didn't know how she would be managing any of this without her parents as well as her sister. Which was a story in and of itself. Lou hadn't been able to count on her sister Marsha for years. Lou would babysit for Marsha's kids but the act was rarely reciprocated. Not that it really mattered— Lou wasn't very comfortable leaving her kids with her self-absorbed sister. She'd worried about their care in her hands. But after a near miss with death, Marsha had changed her stripes. She was becoming a new woman, one who wanted to be there for everyone she loved.

"Can we, Mom?" Emma asked, reminding Lou that Jax was waiting for her answer.

"Yeah, we can. Go ahead and keep right on learning," Lou said, waving a hand toward Emma.

"Emma's got her new songs. I thought I'd take some time with you," Jax said, facing Lou.

With his full attention on her, Lou felt her knees buckle and she fell right back onto the stool behind her. You'd think after a handful of lessons he wouldn't still have this effect on her. But that thought would be wrong.

"Emma, if you want, you can go practice in there." Jax pointed toward the recording room.

Emma's eyes went wider than Lou had ever seen them. "Really?" she asked with a voice full of awe, bordering on reverence.

Jax grinned as he nodded.

Emma stumbled, she was so excited at the chance to use the room with a microphone and amazing acoustics.

Soon she was on the other side of the glass and gave Lou two thumbs up before sitting on the stool and turning her focus to her guitar.

Lou knew from experience that Emma was now in her guitar zone. A meteor could fall from the sky and the girl wouldn't even notice as she worked on her notes. Lou had watched Hazel throw a sandwich over Emma's head toward her intended target, Cash, and Emma hadn't even looked up.

"The song was sounding better those last few minutes," Jax said.

Right. Lou pulled her attention away from her daughter to look at Jax. Not that it was any kind of hardship. Although having him now criticize her wouldn't be fun.

"I'm guessing as a busy single mom you don't have much extra time to practice?" Jax asked.

Was it just in Lou's mind or had Jax emphasized the word 'single'?

Lou shooed that thought away. Her heart was living in hope rather than reality, wishing that Jax had noticed she was an available woman. But most likely, he was just a sweet man who understood that a mom doing everything on her own would surely be busy.

"I could make the time. When the kids are in bed and the house is quiet and lonely."

What had just come out of her mouth? Why was she making herself sound so pathetic? Sure, maybe she really was pathetic, but that didn't mean she had to let the gorgeous man standing next to her know all about it.

"But that time usually belongs to my streaming service and a giant bag of chips."

Lou fought the urge to slap a hand over her mouth. What she'd meant to sound like a good time really sounded worse than her first admission. A giant bag of chips?

"One of my favorite ways to spend my evenings as well," Jax said kindly but he had to be lying. There was no way a man who'd partied with the music world's elite went to Lou's favorite warehouse store to get bags of chips the size of small children.

"But maybe you could sacrifice just ten minutes of that time to the guitar? I'm sure that time is precious but I really think you could become proficient if you set aside daily practice time."

Jax gazed at her with such faith that yes, of course Lou

could do this. She would set aside her ten minutes a day and be ready to back up any vocalist by next month.

Okay, that was taking it too far. But she could at least learn to play the song at hand. The one with only three simple chords.

"Awesome. Let's play that piece once more," Jax said, pulling up the stool Emma had been sitting on so that it was right next to Lou. If he sat on it . . .

Jax sat and sure enough, his shoulder brushed Lou's. How the heck was she supposed to concentrate like this?

Lou had been wondering for some time if she was ready to get back into the dating world. Her best friend, Alexis, as well as her family had been urging her in that direction. Harvey had gotten back out there even before he'd divorced Lou, after all, but Lou didn't want Harvey's actions to dictate her future. So she'd shied away from it. Not that there were men knocking down her door to take her out. The dad of one of Cash's teammates had asked Lou out a few weeks before but Lou had told him she wasn't ready yet. It hadn't helped that Cash, along with the man's son, had stood by watching the awkward exchange.

But now Lou was second guessing herself. Should she have said yes? Because the way her hormones were revving at the starting block with Jax's simple touches, maybe it was time to allow a new man in her life. Definitely not Jax—no way would he be vying for the position—but maybe she should give the dad another shot . . . what was his name again? Lou was pretty sure it was C.J. Or maybe J.C? Lou had always had a hard time with initials as names. Or when last names were first names or first names were last names.

Jax cleared his throat.

Oh heavens, she was still in her lesson. Emma apparently came by her ability to fall into the zone honestly.

Lou began to play as Jax had instructed too many moments before and he watched everything about her. Thankfully Lou had to concentrate on her fingers too much to truly notice Jax but she could feel his gaze almost as if it was a touch. First on her hands, then moving up her arms, and even watching her face. But it was his job as her instructor to notice everything about her playing, right?

"I really think all it will take is a bit more practice now that you're relaxing. Take your time with the guitar. Be gentle yet commanding."

Lou's cheeks warmed as she thought of something—or rather, some*one*—else she'd like to take her time with.

Her crush was getting a little out of control.

Reign it in, girl!

"Mom, we need to go," Emma said, running back into the practice room. "The team will be at the field in five minutes."

Lou's eyes flew to the clock. Sure enough, Emma was right. How had Lou lost track of so much time? And how had Emma come out of her guitar-induced trance to notice the time? Evidently Lou's trance had been even deeper than Emma's. Oh, Lou had it bad. For a man she'd never have. To say Jax was out of her league was the understatement of the year. Jax was the star pitcher while Lou was the old woman sitting in the very last row of the stands, her prime long gone.

"Team?" Jax asked as Lou began gathering her things. She set Jax's guitar carefully back in the case and then not so gently flung her purse over her shoulder, hastily digging through it to find her keys.

"Mom's my brother's soccer coach," Emma answered for them because Lou was too frazzled. This was the longest she'd ever spent in Jax's company. She was going to chalk up her incredibly ridiculous behavior to that.

"You coach soccer too? Super mom," Jax said and Lou, in her Jax-drunk state, swore she heard admiration in his voice.

More likely he thought she had too much on her plate and

probably should give up guitar lessons so she'd stop wasting his time. But she couldn't. Not when Emma was so proud of her.

"They didn't have a coach. My dad used to coach my brothers' teams before he got a new girlfriend, but now he's too busy," Emma explained, all too helpfully.

Yes, Lou was the woman with a giant bag of chips, whose husband got a new girlfriend before he dumped Lou. If Jax thought Lou was a catch before, what did he think of her now?

Lou's sarcastic thoughts ran wild.

"I'm sure Jax doesn't need to know all of this. We'd better go." Lou ushered Emma toward the door before she could share any more unwelcome details.

Thankfully the soccer field was only a two-minute drive away so Lou should make it just as all of the kids got there.

"And your mom stepped up. That's pretty dang cool," Jax said, causing Emma to stop. Even Lou faltered a bit. There was definite admiration in Jax's voice now. She wasn't so Jax-drunk that she could have imagined that.

"Mom's the coolest," Emma said matter-of-factly.

Lou pulled her daughter against her in a kind of weird hug since she had her purse and keys but she couldn't let an exclamation like that go unthanked.

"Emma's the coolest," she countered.

"I am," Emma said with a grin.

"Is the game at the park down the street?" Jax asked.

Emma nodded.

Wait, why was Jax asking where the game was?

"I played soccer when I was your age, Emma. I kind of miss it."

Was Jax dropping hints, angling at an invitation? No . . . he couldn't be.

"You want to come watch? It gets kind of boring but if you like soccer maybe you won't get bored," Emma offered.

If even an eleven-year-old had caught on, Jax had to have been hinting pretty hard, right? But why would he want to come?

"Do you mind?" Jax asked, his gaze lifting to Lou.

"Of course not. We're happy to have you. It should be a blast." Lou gave three answers instead of one. So she was maybe a little more Jax-drunk than she'd first thought.

"Great," Jax said. "I'll see you all down there."

He began gathering his things as Lou just watched. Did the man have nothing better to do? His lessons were probably done for the day but surely a guy who looked like that, and was free as a bird, had plans besides seven-year-old soccer.

Lou shook her head. She really needed to get to the field. Jax might have her intrigued but those boys needed her.

Well, at least their the parents did. The kids tended to run wild until Lou arrived.

"See you," Lou responded belatedly. Way too late. So she added, "And I'll Venmo you for lessons. They were great. It was great."

Shut up, Lou!

"See you," Lou said again.

"You already said that," Emma said as she pushed open the door.

Yeah, she had. Just call Lou a smooth operator.

***

LOU HAD FORGOTTEN that not only did her parents come to these games, but today Alexis was coming as well because Marsha wouldn't be there. Her best friend and stepsister, Alexis, was Margie's daughter. And she didn't quite get along with Marsha. Things weren't as bad as they had been, but it was typically better if they didn't cross paths. So as much as Alexis wanted to be the aunt that came to every game, keeping the peace was more important for now.

So when Jax got to the field and set up his chair beside her family and kids, just behind where Lou was standing as coach, Margie, Bill, Alexis, and Alexis's boyfriend Jared all had questions. None they voiced aloud, thank goodness, but Lou could feel them mentally screaming at her as she tried to keep the wiggly boys sitting next to her somewhat in line.

Georgie was picking his nose but Lou couldn't win every battle.

"You got it, Cooper!" Lou yelled, ignoring the silent shouts as well as the man sitting just behind her.

Jax was getting an all-too-good look at her wide bottom from his seat at booty level. Lou had worked hard to lose some of those extra pounds but she was just going to be one of those women who was blessed with a behind no matter what she did.

Then again, was Jax really spending time looking at her booty? Lou doubted it. He was there for the game, right? Because he missed soccer. And the best way to relive his sports-loving days was watching seven-year-olds play?

Lou was maybe more confused now than she'd been at Jax's studio.

But her thoughts had to stray from Jax as Cooper passed the ball to Cash and Cash dribbled past a defender, Lou cheering loudly for her little boy.

Harvey would have been so proud.

That thought stunned Lou for a moment. It hadn't been the kind of thought she typically had about her ex as of late. Her normal thoughts were along the lines of thinking Harvey was about as high on the idiot scale as one could be because he was missing so much. But this most recent consideration of Lou's had been heartfelt, maybe even a little sympathetic that Harvey was missing such important parts of his kids' lives. He may have only himself to blame, but Lou couldn't help pitying him just a tiny bit for what he was losing.

Cash took a shot on goal but missed, the ball going wide of the small net.

"It's okay, Cash! You'll get it next time!" Jax yelled, startling Lou.

Was this man cheering for her son? And why was her heart pounding so fast?

Lou didn't have to think hard to answer her last question. Because Jax was here at this game, taking the position Harvey should have. Jax, who'd met her kids other than Emma once, was here supporting them. Supporting her.

Try as she might, Lou couldn't figure out any other reason for Jax being there. Missing soccer had been a lame excuse that even Emma had seen right through.

Apparently during her first few lessons, she and Jax had created a friendship of sorts. And when he'd heard Lou had been abandoned in this arena of her life, he was here supporting her. With nothing to gain.

The man was too good to be true.

And still totally out of Lou's league. Maybe they'd be friends for a while, at least until some lucky woman on the island got to call Jax hers, but that was all Lou dared to hope for. Even that seemed like a stretch, Jax's current actions notwithstanding.

The quarter was up and Lou sent in the next wave of kids. With eleven players on the team, Lou could sub out the entire team each quarter so that each kid played half a game, except for the goalie. Whoever played goalie got to stay in for the whole game so that position was changed each game. These kids were still at an age where none of them had designated positions; they all played everywhere, just trying to get a knack for the game.

Cash came to sit beside Lou with the rest of the boys who'd

been in the last quarter. But before he sat on the bench that Lou's dad brought to each game to give the kids a seat near their coach, he turned to give Jax a thumbs up.

"Your guitar teacher was cheering for me," Cash said in his outside voice. Which made sense as they were outside, but Lou kind of wished that he hadn't since the volume of his voice had carried for all of Lou's family as well as said guitar teacher to hear.

"He was. His name is Mr. Jax." Lou tried not to stutter over her words even as her cheeks flamed red.

She wasn't quite sure why she was embarrassed, though. Jax had cheered for Cash. All Cash had done was point it out. But reason defied her because she was still flustered and embarrassed.

Halftime came and went in a flurry of orange slices, sunburnt cheeks, and countless paper cups of water. Then Cash was back on the field.

He made a few excellent plays and Jax enthusiastically noticed each and every one. Cash soon became accustomed to turning in Jax's direction anytime he did anything well, knowing Jax's cheer would be forthcoming.

But it wasn't until there were just minutes left in the last quarter, when the game was almost over, that Lou heard the beginnings of an interaction she'd hoped would never happen.

"Good to see you again, Jax," Lou's father, Bill, said.

Lou couldn't bear to look behind her. Had her dad gotten out of his seat and walked past her kids to stand next to Jax? It was all that made sense, considering where she heard his voice coming from, yet she hoped it wasn't the truth. For her dad to go out of his way like that to speak to Jax was so formal. So . . . for lack of a better word, embarrassing.

Lou's cheeks were going to be a permanent red after this game.

She tried to concentrate on the game—these were her boys—but they continued kicking the ball in the right direction without any guidance from her and the conversation happening behind her was like a trainwreck waiting to happen. Lou couldn't help but listen even when it was the last thing she wanted to do.

"You too, Sir."

It sounded like Jax was standing up. Had he stood up? Why? What was going on?

All of that could be answered—well, except for why—with the turn of Lou's head but she couldn't do it.

"Great move, Preston!" Lou called out, hoping she'd said the right kid's name. That had never been an issue before—she'd memorized all of her players' names during their first practice—but her mind was otherwise occupied at the moment and there were three tow-headed blonds on the team.

When Cash didn't turn her way to correct her, Lou assumed she'd gotten the name right. Thank goodness.

Could the last minutes of this game tick by any more slowly?

"I'm a little surprised to see you here. I didn't realize you knew anyone on the team," Bill said.

Lou wished the earth would open up and eat her whole. How was she supposed to live through humiliation like this? Even the back of her neck was fiery hot.

"I'm actually here to cheer on Cash. Your girls were finishing up their lessons and let me know they were headed here. I played soccer when I was about Cash's age and thought it would be fun to watch a game or two." Jax's voice sounded sure and confident.

Wait, had he said 'or two'? He might be coming back? After all of this?

The man was either psychotic or a saint.

"There is something special about seeing sports through a child's eyes," Bill agreed with Jax.

They were agreeing. That was good. Now if her dad would just go back to his seat or if the game would finally end, Lou might live through this experience.

But the refs made no move to blow their whistles; kids kept kicking the ball. Lou had lost track of what was happening on the field, making her the worst coach of all time. Did they hand out that award at the end of the season?

Oh, Preston had the ball again. Good.

Lou's attention was yanked behind her again as Jax spoke.

No! Stop speaking!

"I agree. As well as watching a fantastic mom coach these sports," Jax replied.

Was he talking about her? Why? What?

Lou had heard the phrase 'blowing your mind,' but now she had officially experienced it.

"Lou is a wonder," her father said. As he should. He was her dad. How would Jax respond? How did she want Jax to respond? Lou had no idea. She had been Jax-drunk and now her mind was blown. She had no hope at a coherent thought.

"I agree, Sir."

Jax had agreed. And called her father *sir* again, which Bill had to be eating up. He loved respectful young men. He'd hated how Harvey had called him 'old man.' It had been a joke, but a rather poor one. One that had gone on for years.

"Have you met my family?" Bill asked.

Nooooo!

Worst case scenario, meet Lou's nightmare. That was what was unfolding. Right behind Lou's head.

Finally the whistle for the game blew—at the very worst time. Apparently Lou's team had won, according to the cheers of the kids surrounding her. She absolutely adored these kids, but would they be quiet for a second so that Lou could hear what was happening with her family? Was Dad introducing Jax to Margie, Alexis, and Jared? It was too much. For a random soccer game, just way too much.

It implied so much.

Jax was a kind man. A friend of sorts. But meeting Lou's family, she could just imagine their implications. The knowing raised eyebrows, the shoulder bumps, ugh!

"Smile, Mom. We won!" Cash cheered.

Right.

Lou pasted a smile on her face and gathered her team around her.

"You all did a great job out there," Lou said, proud of mostly coherent words making their way out of her mouth even as her gaze wandered to where her father, stepmom, Alexis, Jared, Emma, Hazel, and Aiden stood in a half-circle around Jax.

Well, thank heavens no one had been left out.

But seriously? Even her five-year-old had had to join them?

"I loved seeing all of the passing and the team playing." Lou was pretty sure this was what she'd said after the last game but these were seven-year-olds. They probably hadn't paid attention, right?

"Let's do it again next week!"

The boys looked at one another for a second or two, wondering if Lou could really be done. She did tend to get long-winded and this was her shortest speech by a long shot, but after a brief hesitation, no one questioned the unexpected early freedom.

The boys got up, running to their parents before Lou could change her mind. And giving her permission to finally see what was going on with her family.

"Hey Lou," called C.J. (or was it J.C.?).

Lou fought the urge to groan.

Her pasted-on smile was getting quite the workout today.

"Hi—" Lou stopped herself from saying a name. With her luck that afternoon she'd get it wrong.

"Thanks for all you're doing out there with Preston. I've noticed his confidence growing these past few weeks and I can't help but attribute that to you. He's had a hard time of it since my divorce."

Lou nodded, realizing how selfish she was being. Yes, a monumental conversation could be taking place behind her but an important one was happening right here. She needed to concentrate on C.J./J.C. If anyone understood the rocky days after divorce it was Lou.

"They are rough times. But Preston is a delight. I really enjoy coaching him."

That was the truth. And it had been good for Cash to get to know Preston. She'd noticed the two of them talking about their new lives. Not in detail, but Preston had told Cash about his new room at his mom's house and Cash had shared about his dad's new girlfriend.

"It's nice to have someone who understands," C.J./J.C. said. Lou really needed to learn his name.

"I agree. It's a road I'd wish on no one but it does feel a little less lonely when you know you're not the only one traveling it." Lou smiled at the man before her.

He was actually pretty nice-looking, come to think of it. When he'd asked her out before, she'd still been so consumed by grief and anger she hadn't seen much, but now she saw a bit more. Blond hair that curled slightly at the ends, gray eyes, a strong jaw. And for a dad he had quite a nice bod. Maybe not exactly shirtless Jax, but nice to look at. Lou felt like maybe she would be allowed in normal stadium seating if C.J./J.C. was pitching the game.

"C.J!" an older man standing with Preston called out.

Thank goodness. Lou made a mental note. C.J. She could remember it. She would remember it.

C.J. turned to look at the man.

"Preston wants to ride to dinner with us. Meet you there?" the man yelled.

C.J. nodded. "Thanks, Dad!"

The man waved and he and Preston, along with a kind-looking woman Lou guessed was C.J.'s mom, walked toward the parking lot.

"I should let you go," Lou said, taking a step back, anxious to save Jax. From where she stood she could see everyone who had left the field and none of her family nor Jax had done so yet. Something bad was surely happening.

"Right, yeah," C.J. said, glancing back toward his family, who were getting into their car. "But before I do, I just wanted to let you know the offer is still out there. If you are ever interested in going out sometime I think it could be fun." He pushed one of those blond curls out of his eyes, making him look much younger than the three plus decades he had to be.

Lou was flattered. As she should be. A nice, good-looking man was asking her out. One still out of her league, but evidently he wanted to play with her. That sounded wrong. He wanted to date her.

Lou bit her lip. Was she ready to start dating? She had a feeling if she didn't say yes right this second she'd never go on a date with C.J.

But would that be so bad? Maybe not.

Yet she wanted to start dating. And C.J. was a nice guy. He didn't make her heart race like Jax, but no one could compare to Jax.

"I'd love to," Lou replied before she could second guess herself. C.J. was giving her a chance. Shouldn't she do the same for him? Especially considering he was seeing her at her physical worst: no makeup, her brown wavy mess of hair pulled back in a bun that had to have flyaways escaping, a pair of black joggers that had seen better days, and a hoodie that read 'Mom Life.' Yet he was still asking her out.

"Really?" C.J.'s eyes lit with delight.

Okay, this was good. Especially for Lou's ego.

"Yeah." Lou grinned.

"Awesome. I have your number because of the soccer group texts. I'll text you tonight. On a separate thread. I won't text the whole team . . . I'd better go." C.J. began walking backwards, waved awkwardly, and then turned to jog toward the cars.

Lou's grin widened.

C.J. was endearing. And one date didn't mean anything. She'd go and have fun. See what life had to offer a single mom besides late-night streaming and a giant bag of chips.

Oh heavens. Jax.

Lou turned, the field deserted aside from her family and Jax.

None of whom were speaking. Instead they looked like they'd just finished watching a scene play out before them. Much like the one Lou had just lived.

A goofy grin was on Alexis's face, a smirk on Jared's. Her father's head was tilted in confusion; Margie smiled just as widely as Alexis. But it was Jax's face Lou couldn't wait to see and yet she couldn't quite bring herself to meet his eyes. What was he thinking? Why did it matter to her? He was just a friend.

When she finally got the nerve to look at him, he shot her a soft smile. One she had no clue what to do with.

"Did Preston's dad just ask you on a date?" Emma asked, her face twisted in revulsion.

"My friend Preston?" Cash asked.

Okay, no time to analyze Jax. Lou had bigger fish to fry.

"What's a date?" Hazel asked.

"It's when you get married," Aiden explained falsely.

Lou needed to pull on the reins, hard and fast.

"A date is not getting married," she tried to correct her kids. She could not have them thinking she was going to marry Preston's dad.

"But people who date get married," Emma pointed out.

"Some. Some people who date get married," Lou amended Emma's assessment.

"Did you date Dad?" Aiden asked.

"And didn't Grandpa date Grandma Margie?" Hazel asked before Lou could answer Aiden.

"Yes and yes. But I also dated a whole lot of guys who I didn't marry," Lou said.

Alexis snorted before slapping a hand over her mouth. Jax's smile widened. Lou didn't dare look at the rest of the group of adults.

What was she doing?

"Okay, not a whole lot. Just a few. Some guys. I'm just trying to say you don't have to marry every person you date."

"Oh yeah, Brittany has a boyfriend and she's not going to marry him," Aiden replied, naming Jared's young tween daughter and Lou's kids' cousin.

To add to the confusion of Lou's family, not only had Alexis's mom married Lou's dad, but Alexis was now dating Jared, the ex-husband of Lou's sister Marsha. And Marsha and Jared shared two children, Brittany and Peter.

"Britt has a boyfriend?" Jared asked, his eyebrows flying up his forehead.

"Aiden! Were you spying on me and Britt?" Emma accused.

"Let's just calm down a sec," Alexis said to her boyfriend who already had his phone out, ready to call his daughter.

"Britt is going to be so mad!" Emma burst into tears as Aiden looked on, unaffected.

Cash, the smart kid, took a step back from the mess as Hazel went to pat Emma on the back.

"It's okay, Em. Britt is always mad," Hazel remarked.

From the mouth of babes. Although Brittany had had less of an attitude lately, thanks to her mom's change of heart about Brittany's dad and Alexis.

Lou was making her way over to Emma when Bill cried out, "How about cheeseburgers and milkshakes?"

It was the way he'd often handled Lou's and Marsha's childhood fights.

"Yes!" Aiden punched in the air.

"Because I won?" Cash asked.

"Can I get chocolate?" Emma asked, her tears suddenly dry.

Lou wasn't sure what had healed her so quickly, Hazel's comment or the promise of milkshakes, but Lou would take it.

"Of course you can, Honey," Margie said as she wrapped a comforting arm around Emma's shoulders.

"Winner's cheeseburgers," Bill declared as he lifted Cash into the air, prompting squeals of delight.

"I don't like cheese," Hazel piped up quietly.

"Cheese-less burgers for the princess," her grandpa amended.

Hazel nodded with satisfaction and led the group toward the parking lot.

Jared and Alexis were huddled in whispered conversation, walking just behind Aiden. Lou was going to guess they wouldn't be joining the cheeseburger gang.

"We can take the kids if you need some time off tonight, Sweetie," Margie said before not so subtly looking in Jax's direction.

Jax.

Oh dear. He'd just witnessed the mayhem that was Lou's life.

She was amazed he hadn't fled the moment her back was turned.

"We'll bring you home a cheeseburger, Mom!" Emma called back, worries about her cousin long gone.

"And the large fries and a very big brownie milkshake," Cash added.

And with that Jax officially knew all of her secrets.

What was she supposed to say to that?

So she let her family leave, as there was no need to respond, and then turned to Jax.

A still smiling Jax.

Was it a smile to mask the horror he felt? Was he thinking that coming to this game was the biggest mistake of his life?

"I'm sorry about all of that." Lou wasn't even quite sure where to start.

"You have nothing to be sorry for. I haven't been this highly entertained in months."

"Life on the island really is slow," Lou muttered.

Jax chuckled. "You all are much better than anything I witnessed in LA. Actually, the last time I've been this happy was the last time I went home to see my family. One that's a lot like this one you're blessed with."

Could the man stop being quite so perfect? If his words weren't enough, there was his accent and the way his green eyes practically glittered.

"Although I have to say there was one thing I didn't enjoy," Jax said, turning to look at the spot where Lou had stood with C.J. "I want to say I'm happy for you, because you deserve the best, Lou. But selfishly I'm hoping it doesn't work out."

Lou worked hard to keep her breath steady. In and out. Was Jax saying what she thought he was saying? No. It had to be code for something different. Anything else.

"I don't date my students, but as soon as your lessons are done . . ." Jax let his voice trail off.

He was out of her league. She was the old woman in the stands. He was the star pitcher. Not the minor league wannabe but the real deal.

"I'm just hoping I won't be too late," Jax said as he reached for Lou's face, tucking some of those crazy flyaways behind her ear, his touch causing shivers to explore her whole body.

Speak. Words. You need them now, Lou.

"I'm confused," Lou managed.

Not her best line but it got the job done.

Jax burst out into laughter. "Really? Because I was worried I was coming on too strong."

"Nope," Lou shook her head. "Not strong enough."

Jax leaned forward, pressing his lips against Lou's forehead. The shivers were replaced by rockets and missiles. Lou's body felt hot and ready to explode all while being perfectly content.

"I like you, Lou. Everything I see makes me like you more. I want to date you. But I don't date students. It's not right, ethically. At the same time, it's not fair for me to ask you not to date anyone else in the meantime—but I also can't let you date other guys without you knowing that I'll be right in the mix as soon as I can be. I won't stay quiet until then and miss my chance."

Jax took both of Lou's hands. "Was that clear enough?"

Lou nodded, feeling like a deer in headlights.

"Go out with C.J. Have a good time. See what's out there. And even though I have no right to ask this of you, wait to make any permanent decisions, please."

Lou nodded once again. How could she not? She understood Jax's reasons for not asking her out and if it were just her, she would have quit guitar on the spot and cancelled her date with C.J., but Jax was right. Lou was fresh out of a marriage, so she should take her time even if she wanted to jump right into

Jax's arms. And she couldn't stop her lessons yet. Not when Emma was counting on her.

Jax released her hands but she wanted to grab them back. The feel of those guitar-worn calluses on her all-too-soft hands had been exactly what she wanted.

But it wasn't their time. Not yet. So she could wait. She could be patient.

"You go first," Jax directed as he pointed toward their cars, the last two in the parking lot. "I'm afraid if we walk together I'll lose my final grip on my self-control and break all of my rules."

Lou had a hard battle with the temptation to let just that happen.

But she wanted Jax to respect his rules. She wanted to be as accepting of him as he'd been of her.

So she walked away, turning back for one last glance before she got into her car.

Jax waved. Such a simple action, yet it lifted Lou's heart.

She could wait. She could be patient.

Lou had a feeling she'd be repeating those two lines as a mantra for the next however long until she could quit guitar lessons while still being a good mom and date Jax.

Because honestly, that man was more than worth any kind of wait.

CHAPTER FOUR

———

DAX SLAMMED the winning card down triumphantly, causing groans to erupt from all sides of the table.

"I swear you cheated," Bess exclaimed, lightly smacking her husband's arm and causing the others to laugh.

Julia loved seeing this side of Bess. According to her she'd never been competitive, instead relishing when others won, but ever since marrying Dax this competitive well grew from within and losing to Dax was enough to drive her to exclamations and even, one time, tears.

Bess had wondered if she was losing her mind.

Julia thought it was hilarious.

"I'm sure he did." Olivia sided with her sister-in-law.

"He won fair and square," Dean, Olivia's husband, chimed in.

"Maybe game night has gone on long enough?" Gen, Bess's sister interjected and her husband, Levi, nodded in agreement.

"Yeah," Bess conceded as she side-eyed Dax.

Julia covered her mouth discreetly, trying to hide the fact that she was seconds away from bursting into laughter.

As others started cleaning up the cards from their game,

Julia stood and moved to the kitchen to put away the snacks and goodies.

"What can I help you with?" Olivia asked as she joined Julia.

"I think I've got it covered," Julia said, sealing chip bags and putting the veggie tray in the fridge.

Game night had become something of a tradition for Julia and her friends but this had been the first time she and Ellis had hosted in Ellis' home. Typically if Julia and Ellis held a night in for their friends, it was at Julia's house. But Ellis had insisted it was his turn tonight.

"Ellis has quite the set up," Olivia said as she gazed around the kitchen, taking in the gray cabinets and dark gray walls that nearly matched the stainless steel appliances but were in complete contrast to the light reclaimed wood island.

"Right? It's absolutely beautiful," Julia agreed.

Ellis had flown in his personal interior decorator from Nashville when he'd decorated his home and Julia wished she'd met the guy before she'd finished designing her own home. Next time she had any kind of a house project she knew who she was calling.

"Do you need any help?" Gen asked as she came into the kitchen with the other women.

Julia smiled as Olivia chuckled. "Olivia just asked the same thing but I think I'm good. You guys are much less messy than the guys at poker night."

"We aren't that bad," Dax called over his shoulder from where he'd been talking with Ellis and Levi.

"Um, as a person who has had to clean up after said poker night, I disagree," Bess said, joining the rest of the women in the kitchen. "There were as many sticky spots after you all left as there were when my kids were toddlers."

"Right? It's like we leave them alone and they forget how to use napkins," Gen agreed.

"No winning this one, Dax," Ellis chuckled as he slapped his friend on the back.

Dax nodded once. "I'm smart enough to walk away before defeat."

The women laughed as Bess picked up bags of chips and returned them to Ellis' pantry.

"Of course we ask to help but Bess just does," Olivia said as she watched Bess work.

Bess looked behind her. "Oh sorry. Was I not supposed to do this?"

Olivia shook her head. "No, it's absolutely fine. But Gen and I asked to help and Julia wouldn't let us. You just did it."

"Sorry, I tend to be a little overbearing when it comes to cleaning," Bess replied.

Julia grinned. She loved that about her friend.

"How did you know just where to put that?" Gen asked as Bess emerged from the pantry.

"It's where I would have put it. Ellis seems like a smart man, so I assumed he'd have the presence of mind to choose the same spot," Bess said with a smirk.

The women laughed once again and Julia relished the friendships she'd made since coming to the island. Although her relationships with her family were improving, she was grateful for her second family here on the island. She knew if anything went wrong there were at least a dozen people she could call for help and vice versa.

When she'd lived in LA she'd had plenty of people to turn to in times of need, but she paid all of them to be there for her. Here . . . well, here people chose to be there for her, and Julia couldn't thank them enough.

"Ticket sales are through the roof," Dax was saying as the men came into the kitchen as though drawn by a magnet.

Didn't the kitchen always end up as the gathering place?

"Nice." Dean shot a congratulatory look toward Ellis.

"It's been a good year," Ellis said modestly.

Julia was proud of her boyfriend and all he'd accomplished. His music was a part of him and when he allowed the world to see that beautiful part, they reacted. Loving his music, buying his album, and clamoring for tour tickets.

"So when do you go to Nashville for rehearsals?" Levi asked.

Each face in the room turned to Ellis expectantly. Julia was also waiting for the answer to this question. She'd been anticipating this tour for months and she knew he had to be leaving soon; he could only practice on his own for so long. But Ellis seemed to be putting off telling her the exact date of his departure for one reason or another. She knew the tour started in less than three months and a tour of this magnitude required a massive amount of preparation. Much of which would have to happen in Nashville.

"Soon," Ellis said with his drawl that Julia loved so much. "But I'm waiting until the last moment to leave the island. I'm in no hurry to live on the road."

Julia could understand that. Ellis had been on tour for nearly a third of his adult life. He'd talked about the toll it took on him but she also knew it was a necessary part of his job. And while he may not love the touring, he did love the job. In order to do that job well, Julia knew it was imperative that Ellis rehearse with his band as well as handle all the multitude of details required to prepare for all of the shows on the road.

"What are you waiting for?" Julia asked, edging closer to her boyfriend.

Maybe that was a question she should have waited to ask

until they were alone, but it seemed anytime she tried to bring up the tour Ellis put her off. He wouldn't be able to ignore her with this audience, though, so Julia was going to take advantage of it.

"Your mom and sister should be visiting soon and . . . " Ellis' voice trailed off.

It was her. Ellis was waiting on her to be okay without him. And while that was maybe the sweetest thing a man had ever done for her, Julia was also slightly annoyed. This was his career. He shouldn't be putting it in jeopardy for her. Especially without talking to her about it.

"I had no idea," Julia said quietly, leaning against the countertop behind her.

"And this is our cue to see ourselves out. It was a lovely evening. Thanks, Julia and Ellis," Bess said as she began ushering all of the guests toward the front door.

Julia was grateful for her friend. Although it had been her fault for bringing this up in front of the group, Julia now needed a private moment with her boyfriend to discuss their future. His future.

"Ellis, you can't put your entire career on hold for me," Julia said as soon as she heard the door shut behind their guests.

"I don't see it like that, Jules," Ellis said as he moved to stand right in front of Julia, his arms on either side of her, bracing himself on the counter behind her.

"How do you see it?" Julia asked, kind of wishing Ellis wasn't so close. When he was like this she lost all train of thought and her brain could only focus on one thing: getting Ellis' lips on her own.

"I have priorities. I always have. Before, the number one thing on my list was my music and career. Now that number one spot has been filled by the woman I love, and I prioritize her over all else," Ellis said.

Julia closed her eyes. She couldn't think like this. Not with Ellis' chocolatey brown gaze and all of the right words that were causing her to melt right there on the spot.

But she couldn't let him do this for her. Not when she knew how much his music meant to him. Putting off leaving could hurt the entire tour. And for Ellis, music was as necessary as food was for most. He wouldn't survive without it. He might be willing to put his career in jeopardy for her sake now, but what if things went south? What if Ellis didn't perform as well and his fans became upset? What if critics came at him? All for Julia.

He would surely resent her. Heck, Julia would resent herself if that happened. She opened her eyes, needing to see Ellis as she spoke her next words.

"I love that you did that for me. I love you for what you're trying to do." Julia wanted to punctuate her words with a kiss but worried she'd get too involved in that and wouldn't come back to the conversation they were having. A conversation they needed to have. "But you can't wait around for the perfect moment to leave me. Honestly, there won't be one. I'm pretty needy, in case you haven't noticed."

Ellis chuckled, the sound reverberating through Julia since he stood so close.

"I love that you need me," Ellis said before leaning down, his intent clear.

But it wasn't kissing time yet. Julia shifted to let Ellis know the talking needed to continue. He gave a slight nod of understanding before his eyes focused on Julia's the way they always did before he said something important.

"What if you came with me?" Ellis asked, his voice tight, almost as if he was nervous about asking the question.

"Came with you? On tour?" Julia asked.

To say she hadn't thought about going with Ellis would be a

lie. Living apart from him for months on end sounded like a version of hell. But at the same time Julia couldn't see herself going on tour. Sure, she'd be happy to visit him when he had some downtime and would definitely attend a show or ten, but going on the whole tour? That would mean putting her own life on hold for the duration. While she might have done that even a few months ago, now that her niece Wendy had moved to the island, Julia didn't think she could. Wendy had no other family on the island and Julia had turned her back on her family for a long time. She wouldn't make that mistake again.

"Is it that hard to imagine?" Ellis asked when Julia had gone quiet for too long.

"No. It's actually pretty easy to see what would happen. We'd both get awful and too little sleep in hotel beds or on the bus. You'd be running off in about a dozen different directions every day and I'd be patiently waiting for you to come back to me," Julia said. Parts of that scenario sounded terrible, although knowing she'd get to see Ellis daily, even if just for a short time, would make it worth it. If she didn't have someone keeping her on the island.

"When you put it like that . . . " Ellis said, understanding dawning on him.

"It's actually a whole lot more appealing than I made it sound. But Wendy's here . . . " Julia let her voice trail off.

"Wendy who you see about once a week?" Ellis asked.

That was true. "But I'm here if there's ever an emergency," Julia replied.

"Bess or Olivia or Gen or any number of people would be happy to fill in for you," Ellis countered.

That was true as well.

"Are you afraid of being that girlfriend who trails after her boyfriend?" Ellis asked.

Of course he would have picked up on that. Although she

hadn't said anything out loud, Julia had to admit she did take issue with the idea, at least a little. She'd never been the kind of woman to chase after a man, even one who loved her. She didn't want to start now. She'd been around enough of the rich and famous to see those kinds of girlfriends. Number one groupies instead of life partners. A role Julia would never be willing to play.

"What if you weren't just a girlfriend?" Ellis asked, dropping his right hand to toy with a certain finger on Julia's left.

Julia pulled her hand away. "If this is a proposal, I object," she said firmly.

She wasn't the kind of woman who needed a thousand roses or a plane spelling out the question with its trail, but she did need the man she loved to take the time to think through the question, not spontaneously pop it during conversation. While she knew he didn't mean it this way, it felt like he was giving in to arm twisting rather than truly proposing because he couldn't stand to live without her any longer.

"It's not, I promise. When I propose there will be no question in your mind as to what I'm doing. I'm just asking, what if we were married? Would you feel differently about going on tour with me then?"

Her annoyance subsided when she realized Ellis wasn't considering proposing just to get his way. With her irritation gone, she thought about his question carefully. Would she? There was still her concern about Wendy. And although Ellis was right that others could care for her niece and Julia didn't see her all that often, Julia just didn't feel right about leaving. Even if she did have a ring on it.

She shook her head and Ellis sighed.

"I'm honestly thinking about cancelling the whole thing. I don't want to be away from you for so long. The road is always lonely, but now that I've experienced life with you? I don't even want to try it," Ellis said, dropping his chin to rest on Julia's head.

She wrapped her arms around her boyfriend's waist, holding on even as she knew she had to let him go. "But you have to go on tour." She didn't see an alternative.

Ellis straightened and shrugged. "Not every album requires a tour."

"At your level, yes, it does. And on top of that, you're already selling tickets to fans who love you and your music. You can't cancel on them now."

Julia could see the indecision in Ellis' eyes.

"I require you."

"And you'll have me," Julia reassured.

"Waiting at home. I know," Ellis said, a frown marring his lips.

"It will just be a few months."

"Nearly a year," Ellis amended.

Okay, that was a long time. But people did long distance all the time.

"I'll visit you lots," Julia promised.

"It won't be the same," Ellis said, taking a step back.

Julia knew it wouldn't, but what else could they do?

"I get what you're saying, though," Ellis said as he crossed his arms over his chest. "And if the situation were reversed I'd probably need the same thing. If you had to film a movie on location and I had family on the island, why would I leave? You'd be working long days, I'd probably see you for a couple of hours a day if I was lucky, some days not at all."

Julia nodded. That was exactly what her filming schedule had been like.

"It would drive me crazy to just be waiting around for when you were free. You have a life here. Why uproot it all?"

Ellis was voicing exactly what Julia had been thinking. She loved him for understanding.

"It's not that I don't want to go with you," she assured him. "But this is your thing, Ellis. I'll have my things here and then when the tour is done we start our things together again." Even as she spoke, she hated the idea of doing her own thing without Ellis. He'd become such an integral part of her life she wasn't sure how she'd manage to fill the hole he'd leave. But it was what made the most sense. Living on his tour bus for months? Surely that wasn't feasible.

"You have to go, Ellis," Julia said, unwavering on that fact.

Ellis nodded. He knew he did.

"Bill called me today. The band is chomping at the bit to get started . . ."

Julia figured that would be the case.

"But I wanted to at least wait until after your mom and sister come to visit," Ellis added sweetly.

This man was a gem. One she didn't deserve. He knew how hard it was going to be on Julia to spend time with her estranged sister and her mother with whom she'd never really had the best relationship. For him to put off leaving town for that? Man, she loved him.

"You know how it goes, though. Who knows with them? They've cancelled on me twice now. Maybe they won't even make it out here until after the tour is over," Julia said with a roll of her eyes.

Ellis chuckled and pulled Julia in close. Exactly where she loved to be. How could she give this up for nearly a year?

But she'd manage. She'd have to.

"I guess I should schedule my flight then?" Ellis asked, almost as if he hoped Julia would tell him no.

But this was the right thing. Julia hesitated but finally

managed a firm nod. Ellis had to go. His team, fans, and career all deserved it.

Julia opened her mouth to ask him to grab two tickets. She could go along for a few weeks right now, couldn't she?

But her mom and sister were supposed to visit in two weeks. She couldn't be gone for that. And if she started this tour process with Ellis, would she ever come back home without him? She didn't know if she could. And she really should stay in town for Wendy's sake. At least until Julia knew her niece would be just fine without her. And right now she didn't know that.

"I'll miss you," Ellis said, his voice rough and low as he wrapped his arms even more tightly around Julia.

Missing him didn't seem to cover all that Julia would feel.

"Same," was all Julia could manage. She loved this man with every beat of her heart.

"Are you sure I can't cancel the whole thing?" Ellis asked so seriously that Julia had to laugh.

"I'm not joking," Ellis said.

Julia knew he wasn't. That was part of what made it so funny. And it was better to laugh than to cry.

"We'll be stronger for this," Julia said the placating words.

"I'm calling B.S."

Julia laughed once more.

"I should probably leave town in the next day or two," Ellis said into Julia's hair.

Julia bit back a gasp. So soon? She shouldn't be surprised. Ellis probably should have left long before.

"Okay," she managed. She would visit Ellis. And he'd come home if and when he had any downtime. They would make this work.

Thinking about the next time she'd see him helped to ease the sharp ache in her chest.

"I love you," Ellis whispered as he pulled back just enough to look down at Julia's face.

Julia reached up, knowing that kissing time had finally arrived. She didn't want to waste any more time with words. Not when Ellis was leaving so soon.

Ellis knew exactly what she wanted, leaning down so that his lips were within her reach. And she claimed them as hers. All of her was his and all of him was hers. To part while knowing that would be heart-rending. But they'd make it.

Wouldn't they?

CHAPTER FIVE

"I BET I CAN FIT SIX!" Peter exclaimed to his sister around his mouth full of ooey-gooey, half-eaten marshmallows.

"Fine, then I can do seven!" Brittany spouted right back as she quickly began stuffing as many of the white puffs into her mouth as she could.

Alexis sat on the other side of the fire from the siblings, one of Jared's strong arms wrapped around her shoulders.

It was like watching the grossest yet most intriguing game of Name that Tune. Except instead of songs playing at the end Alexis was pretty sure someone was going to end up losing the dinner they'd just eaten. Maybe Alexis.

Jared had installed this firepit in his backyard just a few weeks before and it was officially one of Alexis' favorite parts of his home. The flames that seemed to ignite out of rocks were not only a beautiful feature, but were also practical. With a simple switch the fire sprang to life.

"I can do eight," Peter said, his words muffled.

This was going to be bad.

And yet, as a new addition to a family of teens, Alexis had learned that sometimes you just had to let bad things happen.

The good news of the evening was that Jared was holding her close and no one had yelled that it was inappropriate or that their eyes were going to bleed from the disgusting sight. Alexis was going to count that as a win.

"Are you sure I shouldn't talk to her about it?" Jared whispered into Alexis' ear.

Goosebumps that had nothing to do with the chilly night air erupted over her arms. What Jared had said was far from sweet nothings. He was still trying to convince Alexis that it was a good idea to confront his twelve-year-old daughter about her secret boyfriend, but his breath on the sensitive spot of her ear still thrilled Alexis to her core.

"Yup," Alexis reiterated.

Brittany would come to them when she was ready. It wasn't like she was sneaking out to see said boyfriend. Alexis was pretty sure as a seventh grader the "relationship" was innocent, and why disrupt the happy dynamic they had in their home for a boy Brittany would probably "break up" with in a few days?

She turned to kiss Jared on the cheek, the most she dared in front of his kids, to try to placate him. Jared was the best of dads but tended to be a bit overprotective when it came to his youngest and only daughter.

"What if Peter had a secret girlfriend?" Alexis returned the favor by whispering into Jared's ear.

She enjoyed watching him shiver. She loved that she had that kind of effect on him.

"That's different," he said in a low voice.

"Fine, I'll do nine!" Brittany said—or at least that's what Alexis thought she was trying to say through her sticky, over-stuffed mouth—as she tried to shove another giant marshmallow into the already overflowing space.

"How?" Alexis asked with a raised eyebrow.

"He's older."

Alexis was sure that wasn't the only reason.

"And a boy," Jared acknowledged.

"I get that she's your baby girl, but wait it out." Alexis was pretty sure this was the right course. Not that she knew much about raising tweens. But she had been a tween girl once and she figured that had to count for something.

"Fine," Jared said as he pulled Alexis in a little closer. "Although with the way my hormones are revving at the feel of my pretty woman in my arms I probably shouldn't be giving in. You have no idea what a beautiful girl does to a boy."

Alexis really wanted to turn in her seat and show Jared he wasn't the only one with overactive hormones in this situation but she kept herself firmly in place. She really didn't want to alienate Jared's kids after she'd worked so hard for the little approval they'd given her. Although Brittany and Peter had come to accept that Alexis was now a part of their lives, she was far from their favorite person. Alexis could still count on one hand the number of real conversations she'd had with either child. In the past months of working to win them over, she'd basically graduated from the most hated woman on the planet to a neutral nothing. A huge jump, but still far from where she wanted to be.

"I can do—" Peter began before spewing his marshmallows all over the grass behind the firepit.

Alexis looked away as she heard Brittany's muffled exclaim of, "Gross!" moments before more spitting noises followed.

Brittany was surely losing her marshmallows as well.

"Here." Jared was ready with napkins for both of his kids. Everyone had known what the result of this game would be.

Peter took his first, quickly cleaning himself up before reaching for a skewer. "I guess it's time for s'mores."

Alexis wasn't sure how he still had an appetite for marshmallows, but to each his own.

Brittany wiped her mouth before settling back into her seat with her phone. It had been a gift from Marsha that Jared wasn't too happy about. They'd had a 'no smartphone' rule until the kids were thirteen but Marsha wasn't exactly the rule-following type. Especially when it came to attempts at buying her kids' love.

Peter put his marshmallow-filled skewer right into the flames and pulled out the burning treat before blowing on it and sandwiching it between graham crackers, along with two squares of chocolate.

"Doesn't it just taste like charcoal when you do it like that?" Jared asked his son.

"Just the way I like it." Peter licked his lips before cramming half of his creation into his mouth in one bite.

Jared shook his head, his thoughts probably along the lines of Alexis'. The teen boy brain was an interesting place.

They all enjoyed a quiet moment until Alexis felt Jared shift, turning slightly to face Brittany.

"Who're you texting?" Jared asked, his voice nonchalant, but Alexis could feel the tension in his body as he waited for her answer.

Uh-oh.

But Alexis kept her thoughts to herself.

"No one," Brittany replied quickly, tilting her phone to hide the screen. The smile that had been playing on her lips for the past few minutes vanished.

Shoot. So she was texting her secret boyfriend. At least since she was just twelve Brittany wasn't quite as adept at lying as an older teen would be.

"Oh yeah?" Jared leaned forward in his seat. "That seems like a waste of precious time."

"What?" Brittany raised her head as if she were just registering the conversation. That made sense. Brittany would have typically come up with a better answer than *no one*.

"Why are you texting no one? Does no one text back?" Jared asked.

Peter's head swiveled back and forth as he watched the conversation while chowing down on his smore.

"It's not really no one. It's just not anything important," Brittany said, her attention back on her phone.

Didn't she know she was approaching dangerous territory? *Pay attention, girl!*

Alexis wasn't sure when she'd taken Brittany's side in this but she had. Not that Jared was wrong, necessarily, but Alexis felt Brittany deserved a bit of privacy. It wasn't like she was breaking any rules. As far as she knew, Jared and Marsha didn't have a rule about dating. Their kids weren't allowed to go out without their parents knowing, but texting some cute boy? Alexis was pretty sure they had no rule against that.

"Then why are you spending time texting this not important person?" Jared asked.

"I didn't say the person wasn't important. Just the conversation isn't," Brittany replied.

"So then can I see the texts? Since they aren't important?" Jared asked.

Brittany, Brittany, Brittany. She'd walked right into that one.

"Dad!" Brittany gasped. She was finally paying attention, and Alexis could practically see her mind whirling as she scrambled for a way out of this mess.

"Well, since I pay for your phone, wasn't it a rule that I can check it whenever I'd like? I'd like to check it now."

Brittany slid her phone into the back pocket of her jeans.

"Nice try, kid. Hand it over." Jared held a hand out, palm up.

"This is so stupid, Dad," Brittany said, making no move to get her phone.

"Not stupid. If you don't want to lose your phone you'll give it to me."

"That's not a rule!" Brittany exclaimed.

"Is it not? Well, I just made it one. My phone, my rules."

Alexis worked hard not to cringe. This wasn't what Jared wanted, was it? All for a seventh grade boyfriend?

"Just give him the phone, Brit. Let Dad read your dumb conversations with Ellie and Dana," Peter prompted his sister.

"I wasn't texting them!" Brittany nearly shouted and then covered her mouth with both hands, making it all even worse.

"Then who were you texting?" Peter asked.

It was a well-known fact in the Tuttle home that Brittany only texted her two best friends.

"Leave me alone," she seethed at Peter and then turned to her dad.

"Please don't make me, Dad," she pleaded.

Alexis wanted to butt in, but this wasn't her place. She wasn't a mom—heck, she wasn't even a stepmom. She was a girl-friend. And she needed to remember her role. Yet, she'd come to love Brittany and hated seeing her hurting. Especially over something so silly. What could those text messages possibly say?

Jared held out his hand, flexing his fingers to reiterate that he wanted Brittany's phone in his palm.

Brittany bit her lip before swiping under her eyes. The poor girl was crying.

"Jared," Alexis finally whispered.

Jared turned to face her.

She gave the tiniest shake of her head. She had to stick up for Brittany. This wasn't the way to do it, at least not in her book. If Jared was really worried about Brittany he could talk to her first. Alexis felt a stab of guilt that she'd told him not to say anything. Obviously it was bugging him more than she'd realized. But Brittany should have a chance to say her piece before her phone was snatched away and her texts read. Especially if there really had been no rule in place before this. Alexis could see if Jared and Marsha had already explained to Brittany that her phone wasn't a private zone, that they could and would read her texts and go onto her social media. Alexis knew parents who did that and admired them for it. But Brittany had no idea her dad would read her texts. If it had been Alexis, she would have thought the phone to be akin to a diary, where she could air her private thoughts. So if that privacy was invaded without warning?

Jared's eyes shifted from Alexis to Brittany and then back again, looking torn.

"Do you want to tell me who you were texting instead?" Jared went back to his first question.

Alexis breathed out a sigh of relief.

"Can Peter leave?" Brittany looked back at her brother.

Jared opened his mouth but then shut it. "How about we go in the house? Peter's still roasting marshmallows."

Sure enough, the boy had his skewer once again filled with white puffs. Or at least they had been white before he blackened them. He was going to be on a sugar high for days.

Brittany nodded as she stood and Jared did the same.

Alexis wasn't sure what to do. She considered joining them, as Brittany had only asked Peter to leave, but that wasn't the same as witnessing the conversation simply because she was already there. After an internal battle, Alexis stayed seated. If Jared wanted her along he'd say so.

Jared and Brittany started toward the back door.

"Are you coming?" Brittany turned to ask Alexis in an uncertain voice.

Alexis worked hard not to react. She alternated between

wanting to cheer and dropping her jaw in shock. She settled on serene neutrality, or what she hoped was serene neutrality. Playing it cool always worked with tweens, didn't it?

"Do you want me to come?" Alexis asked, hoping she sounded so very cool. Even as she sought to appear nonchalant she needed Brittany to know she had the right to make this decision.

Brittany nodded.

Alexis struggled not to leap up and do a little jig. This was huge for her. For them.

When Brittany wasn't looking Jared turned around to grin at Alexis.

A surge of relief flowed through Alexis. For a few moments there she'd thought he was mad at her. He'd have every right to be, considering she'd been the one who told him to not talk to Brittany and now they were here. She'd also wondered if he thought she'd overstepped by entering the conversation.

But all was good. Better than good: Jared was happy with her and Brittany had asked her to join them. But this was still a serious moment and Alexis was an adult. She'd save her celebrating for later.

Jared closed the back door behind them and led the way to the cozy sectional in the living room. Brittany chose the seat at the end closest to the kitchen, perching on the edge of the cushion, and Jared and Alexis made themselves at home in the large square that combined the two sides of the couch.

Brittany's eyes were on her feet, her breath coming quickly as she waited for her dad to speak.

"Britt, I'm sorry for my display out there. I shouldn't have demanded your phone like that. But I do think we need to set new ground rules with your phone. You got it a year before I was expecting you to and because of that we didn't get a chance to discuss boundaries ahead of time. But a phone is a huge responsibility. Too many kids have complete free rein on theirs and I don't want to do the same with you kids."

"Peter doesn't have rules," Brittany said suddenly, lifting her gaze from her feet to accuse her father.

"Every rule I set into place right now will apply to both of you. Peter got his phone during a crazy time in our lives. I should have set rules for him as well."

Brittany nodded and dropped her eyes again, but at least seemed a little satisfied that she wasn't the only one being held to this new standard.

"Those are my phones." Jared pointed to Brittany first and then out the window toward Peter.

Brittany looked up again. "But it was a present for my birthday. Mom said it was mine."

Alexis scratched her head. This was tricky, but she had faith that Jared could handle the situation.

"It was. I'm sorry that your mom said it was your phone. She should have discussed it with me before she said so," Jared explained, sounding very rational. Alexis hoped Brittany thought so as well. Although she couldn't ever remember describing her mom's lectures as "rational" while receiving them.

"Are you going to discuss these rules with Mom before you say so?" Brittany countered. That girl was too smart for her own good.

But she had a point. Although with a bit too much sass

Jared looked to Alexis. She could see the emotions warring within him. He wanted to lash out at Brittany, to forcibly remind her that he was her authority. But he was making a valiant effort to hold back. To keep his frustration in check.

She watched as he drew a deep breath in and then let it out.

"I don't appreciate the cheek," Jared said as he gripped his thighs with his hands.

Brittany must have realized she'd pushed too far because her lips pressed down into a frown of contrition.

Jared continued, "But I'll talk to your mom."

Brittany turned to Alexis. "And Alexis too?" she asked. This time none of the earlier sass was in her tone.

Alexis felt her eyes go wide.

"You'd like Alexis to be a part of the conversation?" Jared asked, masking his shock better than Alexis did.

"She's not our mom, but she's an adult in our family. She should have a say too, right?"

Alexis was sure this was just because Brittany thought Alexis was going to be on her side but at the moment she didn't care. She wanted to cheer from the rooftops. Brittany had said Alexis was a part of their family!

"You're right. I'll talk with Mom and Alexis."

Alexis noticed Jared was careful not to imply that he'd speak to them at the same time. She could imagine Marsha's reaction would be less than favorable if Alexis joined any parenting conversation. But Alexis didn't care about having any sort of a say in the final decision. The fact that Brittany wanted her to join, that she was considered a part of the family, was way more than enough.

Brittany stood, a confident smile on her face.

"Not so fast. The phone conversation is going to happen in the future but we still have one point I'd like to go over tonight. Who were you texting?"

Brittany shifted from one foot to the other.

"And before you consider lying remember that I could be checking all of your texts in the next few hours," Jared added.

Brittany swallowed before answering, "A boy I know."

"What's his name?" Jared leaned forward so that his fore-arms rested on his thighs.

"Drake," Brittany replied softly.

"And what is this boy to you?" Jared pressed.

Brittany bit her lip as she looked up at her dad.

"Don't lie, Britt. And don't even think that you can erase all of your texts. If I find out you did that, you will be in so much more trouble," Jared said.

Alexis silently cracked her knuckles. She hated this kind of tension.

"He's my boyfriend," Brittany finally admitted, her gaze once again on the carpet at her feet.

"And what does that mean?" Jared asked as he scrubbed a hand over his chin.

"I like him and he likes me," Brittany mumbled.

"Do you go on dates?" Jared asked.

"What? No! That's so stupid, Dad," Brittany replied as her head snapped up, her face full of revulsion.

Alexis tried not to smile. She'd been right. It was all so innocent. Brittany couldn't even imagine a date with her "boyfriend."

"So what *do* you do?" Jared asked.

"He texts me funny memes and I tell him they're dumb," Brittany said.

Alexis covered the start of a giggle with a cough. That sounded so much like Brittany there was no way it could be a lie.

"Is there anything else?"

"He's not allowed to text other girls," Brittany replied with a shrug.

Jared nodded as if appeased by that answer but at the same time seemed deep in thought as he tried to come up with his next question, knowing he probably just had one shot at this conversation.

"So you don't kiss him?" Jared asked finally.

"I don't even see him, Dad!" Brittany said with a roll of her eyes that was so extreme it made Alexis' eyes hurt. "Besides, not every couple is as gross as you and Alexis. Needing to kiss every two seconds."

Brittany rolled her eyes once more and Jared seemed to relax after her latest answer. Alexis was pretty sure that Jared's worst nightmare was that Brittany could already be kissing boys.

"Is that it?" Brittany asked, tapping her toe on the ground.

Jared considered his daughter in silence for a moment, then looked to Alexis, seeming to ask her if there was anything she wanted to add. If Alexis was being completely honest, she did have one question she was surprised Jared hadn't asked: how had Brittany met this boy? But considering how innocent all of her other answers had been, she wasn't going to press just for her own curiosity's sake. Brittany had been through enough.

So Alexis just nodded. Besides, it would have been nearly impossible for Alexis to speak; she was barely containing her mirth over the whole situation as it was. Even though Brittany was so full of attitude she might just explode with it, she was also darn funny.

Jared met his daughter's eyes for a long moment before saying, "For now."

Brittany, freed, immediately dashed out of the room, phone securely in her pocket.

As soon as the girl was out of earshot Alexis finally let out the laughter she'd been holding in for so long, her stomach hurting after a minute of straight giggles.

Jared joined her for part of it but stopped long before she did.

"You can say it," he said when Alexis' laughter finally died away.

"What?" Alexis asked, her eyebrows furrowed in confusion.

"You were right and I was wrong. A boyfriend in seventh grade is definitely not something I needed to worry about,"

Jared replied. His face was adorable when it was full of contrition.

But as cute as Jared was, Alexis couldn't accept it as quite that black and white: him being wrong and her being right. There were some moments during that conversation that Alexis had been sure she was wrong. "Yeah. Thank heavens I ended up actually being right about that. I was worried for a bit there," she replied with a sigh. "I've decided from now on that when it comes to big parenting issues I'll keep my big yap shut."

Jared immediately began shaking his head.

"Please don't. And not just because you were right this time. I need you in this, Lex. Parenting is the hardest thing I've ever done and although I need to do it with Marsha I *want* to do it with you. I want your opinion on things. I love seeing into your brain and your heart with the choices that you make. I love that you love my kids enough to care."

"Really?" Alexis scooted to sit flush against Jared's side.

Jared saying he wanted to parent with Alexis meant the world to her—it would bring her even closer to Jared and his kids. And although she wanted nothing more, she needed Jared to be sure he wanted Alexis along for the ride, even when things got really hard or Alexis was really wrong.

Jared nodded. "Really."

"Okay. Then I guess that means I really am an adult in this family," Alexis beamed as she used the title Brittany had gifted her.

"Wasn't that crazy? When she said that I was so excited I about wet myself in glee," Jared exclaimed happily and then pursed his lips. "Yeah, that line definitely sounded better in my head."

Alexis laughed at the strange sentiment but she got it. She'd kind of felt the same way herself.

"Your kids are accepting me," Alexis said, a smile of relief and joy curving her lips as she leaned her head against Jared.

Jared opened his arms, probably wanting to show Alexis just how accepting he could be, and there was nowhere else she wanted to be. She leaned into Jared's embrace just before the backdoor suddenly slammed open, causing Alexis to jump out of Jared's arms before she'd even fully moved into them.

"I just ate eleven s'mores. I think I'm going to be sick," Peter muttered, holding his stomach as he made his way past the couple toward his room.

Jared hardly even seemed to notice his son as he closed the distance between himself and Alexis. "Now where were we?" he murmured into her ear.

Alexis furrowed her brows. Had Jared just missed that whole scene when his son had walked through the room looking the worse for wear? Peter's coloring had been strange and she couldn't help but feel concerned. "Don't you need to check on him?"

"Self-inflicted sickness in the name of being a dumb teenager is a two on my importance scale. You being ready to kiss me falls way higher than that. Peter will be fine," Jared said as he pulled Alexis closer.

Alexis figured as dad Jared knew best so she wouldn't argue with him. Besides, they had celebrating to do. Alexis had been accepted as a member of the Tuttle family.

CHAPTER SIX

NORA SAT before her most recent watercolor painting that she was creating for Amber and Elise's client, Genevieve. The girls were planning her wedding and Nora was in charge of contributing to the centerpieces: original artwork of photography prints Genevieve had taken with her fiancé. Which were turning out rather nicely, if Nora did say so herself.

And thank heavens they were, considering the small fortune Genevieve was paying Nora. It was a lot of work, but Nora had been able to take the time off from her day job at the gallery her sister owned. So now Nora got to live the dream of painting full-time for gobs of money. Her only concern was a niggling worry that Genevieve might not like the paintings. But she pushed that thought away. It never served her to worry about a client while she worked.

Instead, Nora turned her thoughts to the other wedding. Amber and Raul were still on track to get married and the date was approaching quickly . . . too quickly. Nora had thought about bringing up her concerns that Amber was only choosing Raul because he needed her and wouldn't leave her. After their conversation in Seattle, Nora knew Amber's abandonment issues could still be a problem. But as Nora had thought about it, she'd come to the decision that if Amber really felt that way, it was something she'd have to discover about herself on her own. It definitely shouldn't come from the woman who'd first abandoned her. However noble Nora's motives for allowing Amber to be adopted may have been, in the end, it still would have appeared to Amber as abandonment. At least to a girl in her formative years. So Nora had decided it was up to her to just be supportive about this wedding. A shoulder to lean on. If Amber ever shared those concerns with Nora they'd talk about it, but until then it seemed there was enough for Amber to ponder over.

"She chose my florist!" Amber rushed into Nora's makeshift studio, triumphant.

At the sudden interruption, Tabby jumped in the seat she'd taken in the corner of the room. She'd come to love the window-filled room almost as much as Nora did and could often be found reading in that corner.

After Tabby settled, she and Nora exchanged a look Nora had just learned. The one that said, *I have no idea what's going on but I will be excited for my child.* Nora had dang near perfected it thanks to the wedding planning process they were all enduring—that is, enjoying.

"Remember how I gave Genevieve three florist options?" Amber asked, looking from her mother to her birth mother and squinting because of the sunshine.

It was a bright, light day on the island of Whisling and Nora was trying to take advantage of every moment. Since she'd moved to the island she'd learned to paint in less light than she was used to down in San Diego. Whisling just had more cloudy days than, well, practically the rest of the United States. Not great for an artist. But then again, once Nora had gotten used to painting in the new kind of light she had found that it had helped her to see her art in a different way and she was grateful for the change. But despite learning and enjoying how to paint with more of a gray sky, she still relished a good sunny day.

Tabby nodded and Nora realized she had yet to answer Amber's question. So she nodded as well. Of course they knew about Genevieve's florist options. They knew nearly as much about Genevieve's wedding planning as Amber's. For some reason the two weddings seemed to overlap more than one would expect.

And if one wedding to plan was overwhelming, two were infinitely more so. Nora was so grateful Tabby was with her for it. Amber had leaned on her moms and Nora felt she would have buckled if she'd been on her own. But thankfully Tabby had come back to the island after their weekend in Seattle for just this reason. She'd be leaving for home in just a few days and Nora wasn't sure how she'd cope on her own. But Tabby had already been away from home for much longer than they'd initially expected.

Nora was pretty sure the impromptu trip had been planned after Elise had told her parents that Amber had been considering eloping. Elise, Tabby, and even Gerry seemed to have decided to put up a united front of support, none of them voicing their opinions on how fast everything was moving. And in response Amber had reset her wedding date for November, the original plan, instead of moving the date up like she'd been thinking about doing when she'd considered eloping.

Everyone was making concessions, and it seemed that the truce was working for now.

"So two of the options are in Seattle, and I thought for sure Genevieve would go with one of them because they have gorgeous blooms and way more stock than our little Whisling florist has. But because it would be easier for all if we went with a local florist I approached Nikki, the owner of Whisling Florist and told her everything we needed from her if she wanted to be in the running for the job. She seemed willing and able to do all that the Seattle florists would have provided. She promised that she could get the exact blooms for the arrangements Genevieve wanted. She said she'd even hire more help just for the day of the wedding to make sure everything went according to Genevieve's wishes. It will cost Genevieve a bit more to get the flowers to the island but in the long run it will actually cost less than the other florists because transporting entire arrangements from Seattle will be even more expensive. Although we all know how little Genevieve considers money when making wedding decisions," Amber explained, filling in Nora and Tabby on all the details.

One never knew which way things would land when Genevieve made choices. Neither money nor convenience seemed to affect her. Money she had plenty of and convenience was a perk that went along with money: she paid other people to deal with the inconvenience. But for Amber and Elise it was a big deal because they were often the ones to struggle with the inconveniences. Yet even if Genevieve always chose the most difficult option, it would all be worth it in the end. So Elise and Amber accepted her decisions without complaint, even as they wished she would choose differently, because they knew they had been gifted a blessing when Genevieve, the Hollywood diva, decided to have her wedding at their little inn on Whisling Island. The media coverage the event would surely bring would put their fledgling business on the map, not to mention the many rich and famous who would get firsthand experience at the inn as wedding guests.

"But she chose Nikki! She loves the idea of the florist being local. She called it 'small town quaint,'" Amber quoted and Nora could almost hear Genevieve say it, her impression was so spot on.

Tabby clapped happily as Nora beamed. They still weren't sure why choosing the local florist was so important to Amber but they'd learned during the wedding process to cheer first, ask questions later.

The door behind Amber suddenly opened and Elise poked her head in, seeming shocked by how full the room was.

"What are you all doing back here?" she asked as she entered the awkwardly shaped room in the back of the inn.

So far the girls hadn't found a long-term use for the space because it was so strangely shaped and hadn't been remodeled with the rest of the place. The floors were still the original wood, in workable condition but very worn, and the walls had chipping yellow paint. But none of that mattered since two of the walls had nearly floor-to-ceiling windows. Nora wasn't sure what the old owners had used this space for but when she'd been hired to paint for Genevieve's wedding she'd instantly known she wanted this exact spot for her studio. Thankfully Amber and Elise had been more than willing to let Nora use the space.

"Mama Nora's painting," Amber said, pointing to the easel carrying Nora's latest rendition of Genevieve and her groom. The end result was pretty dang stunning, even if Nora felt a bit guilty thinking that about her own work.

"I get why she's here, but what about the rest of you? Doesn't she need to concentrate?" Elise looked at Amber and then Tabby accusingly.

Nora grinned at her second daughter's protectiveness. Although Amber was technically the only member of their family who was related to Nora, as Nora had gotten to know Amber's adoptive family, she had come to love Elise as her very own as well. Tabby saw this, and thankfully, ever gracious, she didn't seem to mind sharing her daughters with Nora. She had fully embraced Nora as a member of their family, and Nora couldn't have felt more blessed that they were the family that had adopted Amber.

"I was reading silently in that corner." Tabby proclaimed her innocence as she pointed to the plush chair she'd brought into the room when she'd first joined Nora a few days before. The moms had realized that being in the same place helped in wedding planning. Amber would then just have to come here to find both of them. Tabby had also told Nora that the peace in this space when Nora painted was something she'd craved for years. The smell of paints calmed Tabby as it did Nora, so the two of them had been sharing the space happily. Sometimes they'd talk but most of the time, as Tabby had said, she'd be in the corner reading while Nora painted.

"And I had to come tell them that I got the florist!" Amber exclaimed.

"The florist?" Elise asked.

Amber nodded and Elise took her sister's hands as the two began jumping in unison.

"Half-price flowers!" Elise cheered.

"Half-price flowers!" Amber echoed.

Nora had a feeling they were getting close to the part of the story where she would understand why Amber was so excited about this florist, but they weren't quite there yet. Tabby raised an eyebrow, showing her confusion as well but both moms waited patiently for the details to unfold.

"That's why I was so excited when Genevieve chose Nikki. Nikki had let me know that if she got to do the flowers for Genevieve's wedding she'd give me a huge discount for mine," Amber explained with a giddy grin. "I was worried that wasn't ethical but I told Genevieve after she chose Nikki that I'd been offered that deal and Genevieve was thrilled for me. She said I deserved it after the wonderful job we were doing for her."

"Eek!" Amber squealed, jumping once more.

"So you're getting the roses then, right?" Elise asked, her eyes bright with excitement.

Over the past couple of weeks Nora had seen a change come over Elise. Nora wasn't sure if Elise was putting the situation with Raul from her mind, not allowing herself to worry that the man might just be using Amber, or if she was genuinely accepting him as Amber's choice. But whatever she was doing, it was working for Amber. Ever since their weekend in Seattle, Elise had dived head first into wedding planning, exactly as Amber had been hoping when she'd announced her marriage plans.

"I don't know. They are still so expensive . . . " Amber hemmed.

"But at half price they are nearly the same price the daisies were going to be, right?" Elise asked.

"But now I could get the daisies for super cheap," Amber pointed out.

Elise shook her head as she turned to Tabby. "Dad would want Amber to have the roses, right?"

Tabby scratched her nose, her lips pursed.

"Dad would want the cheaper option, wouldn't he?" Amber asked with raised eyebrows.

Tabby nodded at Amber, acknowledging that she was right.

"But," Tabby interjected before either girl could speak, "your father and I are footing the bill together. And *I* want you to have the roses."

Nora still felt a twinge of guilt whenever she thought of the price tag on this wedding. She'd wanted to help with the cost, but Tabby and Gerry wouldn't hear of it. They'd been saving for Amber's wedding all of her life, they told her, the same as they had for their other children, and as much as they appreciated Nora's offer of help, this was something they insisted in doing on their own. They gave Nora no room for argument so she'd had to give in. But she'd immediately started planning a beautiful painting as a gift for the parents of the bride on the special day. That helped to placate her guilt . . . somewhat.

Amber's eyes lit up before she began jogging in place, too excited to keep still. "The roses? Seriously?" Amber squealed. Elise echoed the sound. "I'm just so excited I don't know what to do!" Amber said. "I need to tell Raul!"

Still jogging, she whirled and left the room.

Elise giggled before turning to Nora and Tabby.

"You made her day," Elise said brightly to her mom.

Tabby nodded, but now that Amber was gone her underlying concern was etched all over her face.

"We're doing the right thing, aren't we?" she asked Elise, turning to Nora to show the question was for both of them.

Elise's smile dipped a bit but didn't disappear. "The alternative isn't an option," she said softly, reminding them of Amber's determination to elope if they didn't support her. Missing her big day would cause a rift in their relationship with her that they weren't willing to accept. "There is no right thing, because there's only one thing we can do."

Tabby nodded slowly, her lips still pursed. She understood this and was trying hard to play her part, however, they were all still a bit uneasy. But Elise was right. There was no choice for them. They had to either support Amber or miss her wedding. The latter wasn't an option so they had to do the former.

"I get that. And I'm trying," Tabby said softly.

"We know, Mom. You gave her the roses." Elise grinned and Tabby returned her grin. Nora wished Amber's wedding planning could have been more joyful all around, but at least they were finding little moments of happiness.

"I do need to voice one last concern now that Amber isn't around," Tabby said slowly as if she was wishing she didn't have to say something but knew she should. To be a good mom. "Have you looked into your business agreement with Amber?"

Elise's grin suddenly disappeared, fully this time. "With a lawyer a few days ago," she said quietly. "If Amber refuses to sign a prenup and Raul chooses to divorce her we could lose up to half of the inn because of the wording in our contract. We are joint owners but we didn't divide up our stake in the inn, so if Raul found a really great attorney he could use our contract and say that technically Amber owns a hundred percent of the inn. We didn't think at the time it was important to clarify our stakes."

Elise bit the inside of her lip as Nora stared at her, speechless. She'd had no idea Elise stood to lose so much with this wedding. Yet, she hadn't said a word of it to Amber. All of her concerns had been for Amber's sake, not her own.

"Hopefully if it comes to that we'll find the better attorney," Elise said cheerfully. She was clearly working hard to hide her worries and Nora's heart hurt for the sweet woman.

"We'll make sure of it," Tabby promised her daughter as she put an arm around her shoulders.

Thankfully Elise had the same support that Amber did, including Nora's. Nora nodded in agreement with Tabby's declaration to show that she'd be there, searching for the best attorney, as well.

Elise nodded. "And that is absolute worst case scenario. If we're at that point, the inn will be my last worry. I'm sure I'll have a distraught sister, and she matters so much more."

Elise's response was almost unbelievable. How could someone be so selfless? As worried as Nora was for Amber's marriage, she knew Amber was still in a better place than most. With family like this, Amber was one lucky woman.

"I FEEL like I haven't seen you in weeks," Nora said as she opened the front door to her condo and Mack walked in.

He immediately enveloped her in a hug and Nora breathed in the cedar and spicy scent that was all Mack.

Holy moly, she'd missed this man. But between his covering her shifts at the gallery and her hours spent painting, as well as wedding planning with Amber, they'd been like two ships in the night.

"What do you say we both quit our jobs and run off to some tropical island?" Mack murmured into her hair, still holding her tightly.

"Give me five minutes to pack a bag," Nora replied even though they both knew it would never happen.

Mack smiled before pressing his lips against Nora's forehead so that she could feel his joy at their being together.

He let her go and Nora wanted to shout her displeasure but they couldn't very well hug and kiss in her entryway all evening. They had to at least move to her couch.

But when Mack took a slow step backward, that was not okay. "Where are you going?" Nora asked, only a little ashamed of how shrill her voice sounded. But Mack had better not be leaving.

"Just right here," he promised as he motioned to the left of the doorframe, just outside the door.

When he came back into view he held two bags as well as a gorgeous bouquet of orange, yellow, and red fall wildflowers.

"Oh, they're beautiful," Nora said as she took in the blooms, bending her head to sniff the fragrance. There was nothing like the beauty of fall. "Thank you," she said before kissing Mack to show her gratitude.

Mack tucked his free arm around Nora's waist, pulling her closer, and she knew he was about to deepen the kiss. She desperately wanted him to do so, but exercising all of her restraint, she stepped away. They'd been in this exact same situation one too many times and Nora had always chosen kissing over all else. It worked well for a while but then hanger would hit and, well, Mack didn't do well without food. She'd learned that if she wanted an optimal kissing experience with Mack it was better to eat first and enjoy him later.

"We have to eat soon," she said, pointing to the bags of food in Mack's hand. "I'm guessing you haven't eaten in at least three hours and that means we have about five minutes before you go hungry Godzilla on me."

"Hey, there are more ways to fill me than with food," Mack said with a wink, his voice as smooth as his moves.

Nora felt her core warm and was about to throw all of her earlier caution to the wind when her phone rang.

She stepped back.

"Get it," Mack said, even as disappointment filled his features. This evening was supposed to be about the two of them but he knew as well as Nora did that the melody filling the room was Amber's ringtone.

Nora hesitated.

"It's fine," Mack promised, smirking to show Nora that he really was okay.

But that smirk was Nora's kryptonite and made her want to do the opposite of what Mack has suggested. She wanted to ignore the call and . . . but she really should answer the phone. It was Amber, after all.

Resigned, she pressed the accept call button.

"Hey," Nora said breathlessly into the phone. She hoped her daughter couldn't hear it on her end.

Nora flopped onto the couch, mostly to get away from Mack. If she stayed near him she wasn't sure even having her daughter on the phone could keep her from throwing herself at her boyfriend.

"Hi Mama Nora!" Amber said brightly and all of Nora's frustration at being interrupted melted away. "We're having an impromptu wedding planning meeting at our place and wondered if you wanted to join. We figure since Mom will be leaving the island soon we should get as much done as we can first."

That made sense, it really did. But did they have to meet that night? She couldn't leave Mack. Not after promising him this time together. Not when she ached to be with him. But then again, how could she say no? Amber would be able to plan without her but she would surely feel a little disappointment.

"Go," Mack mouthed.

Of course he did. Because he was the most understanding man on the planet.

Nora shook her head. She was eighty percent sure she should stay with Mack. Their relationship needed time together.

"You should go," Mack said, this time saying the words aloud.

"Is that Mack I hear? Tell him to come too. Raul should be coming by at some point. We're going to order pizza and make a night of it," Amber said.

Nora met Mack's gaze. He was somehow smiling even before he nodded. "I'd love to see your girls."

"See, he wants to come. Bring him," Amber said as if it had been a foregone conclusion that Nora would be joining them, and the only question was whether Mack would too.

Mack was already putting their Thai takeout in Nora's fridge along with Whisling Bakery's chocolate fudge cake that Nora was obsessed with. He'd gotten all of that? For her? He hadn't even asked what they should eat; he'd just gone to her favorites even though Nora knew Mack preferred sushi to Thai curry and caramel to chocolate.

"I love you," she mouthed when Mack turned back in her direction walking toward the couch.

"I know," he mouthed back.

Nora grinned. She was literally the luckiest woman on the planet.

"See you in twenty?" Amber asked, knowing that was how long it took Nora to drive from her place to the inn.

Nora might have to give up most of her alone time with her hot boyfriend that evening but . . . "Make that thirty." She hung up and pulled Mack onto the couch beside her.

She was about to make really good use of those extra ten minutes.

CHAPTER SEVEN

LOU HAD LEARNED a lot about patiently waiting since she'd last spoken to Jax. Specifically, that patiently waiting stank. Stank like funky garbage on a hot summer's day.

For too many moments of each day since that soccer game Lou had alternated between wondering if that conversation with Jax in the park had really happened to trying to figure out any kind of sneaky way to get out of being his student. Jax would marry parents of his students, right? Oh heavens. Had she thought marry instead of date? Lou was worse than her children.

But when she had finally gathered up the courage to talk to Emma about the possibility of quitting, prepared with her speech that Emma would be free to continue but maybe Mom should try something else, Lou had only managed the words 'guitar lessons' before Emma had interrupted. She'd gushed on and on about how fun it was that they were taking lessons together and how amazing it was that Mr. Jax taught both of them. She never thought she'd have the same teacher as her mom and wasn't it so fun?

Lou had forced herself to reply that yep, it was super fun

before going to her room to lick her wounds. Really, she was thrilled Emma was so happy and in her element. The divorce had been harder on her than the other kids.

But why had Lou signed her up with lessons from Jax of all people? Granted, she would probably never have gotten to know Jax were it not for the lessons. Ogling him from afar at the gym would have been her closest interaction. Without lessons, she would never have had the nerve to talk to a man who looked like Jax.

And the problem was even with how droolworthy he was, Jax's appearance was one of the least attractive things about him. He was kind and gentle with Emma as well as Lou. He never seemed to judge her, even during their first lesson when she'd cried as Emma first started playing or when she almost aways arrived to lessons with a rat's nest of hair on her head. She was an emotional and physical wreck but he'd always been so understanding.

And now she knew that gracious, supremely hot, and nearly perfect man wanted to ask her out. Her! Lou.

Yet here she was getting ready for a date with another man.

The universe was a strange place sometimes.

"So if you go on two dates with Preston's dad you'll marry him?" Hazel asked from her perch on Lou's bed, her head cocked adorably.

Her question? Not so adorable. Lou didn't want her kids to get it into their heads that she was marrying Preston's dad. Because Jax was right. She should get some dating experience under her belt. Her last date had been with Harvey, way too many years before. And the good thing about Preston's dad was that the guy seemed to be dating for the exact same reason. Lou got the vibe that he wasn't super into her. It was more *I'm here, you're here, why don't we go out?*

"No," Lou said as she held up a light blue button-up still on the hanger over her body. Why had she ever bought light blue anything? The color did nothing for her complexion.

"After how many dates then?" Hazel asked.

"I'm not marrying—" Lou began when Cash sprinted into her room, skidding to a stop just before he ran into Lou's wooden bedframe. That could have been a terrible collision.

"Ten," he declared confidently.

Where had he been and how had he heard Hazel's question?

Lou's children never ceased to amaze her. And terrify her.

"So after ten dates you'll marry Preston's dad. Will Preston be my brother?" Hazel asked as she pushed herself off of Lou's pillows and sat on the edge of the bed, her little feet swinging. Cash joined her.

"No. I'm not marrying Preston's dad," Lou said with finality as she held up a yellow blouse and gazed into the mirror. Better but still not great.

"How do you know?" Emma asked, joining the rest of them.

Why were all of her children hearing *this* conversation?

Lou had given a speech about cleaning up after themselves in the bathroom the day before. She'd even sat all of them down on the same couch for it and still three of them had had to ask Lou to repeat herself multiple times before the message got through.

"How do I know what?" Lou hedged as she set down the yellow shirt and sprayed some dry shampoo into her roots. Her hair was looking a little sad and saggy.

"That you won't marry Preston's dad?" Emma pressed.

"Because . . . " Lou searched for an answer that was acceptable for young ears. Her mind supplied plenty of reasons. Because the man, while nice, didn't cause butterflies in her belly or sparks on her skin. Because Lou didn't want to be in another marriage where the man was just acceptable. "It doesn't feel like

I'm going to marry Preston's dad. And for the really big decisions in life, like getting married, they have to make sense in your head *and* your heart."

Go Lou! That was definitely some of her best work in a long time. She was grateful to note that Emma was quiet, seeming to ponder over her words.

Yes, those are good ones, dear daughter. Ponder them, treasure them, use them when you are old and gray.

Still proud of herself, Lou put on one last swipe of lipstick before grabbing the yellow top. Better but not great would have to do.

"But why are you going on a date with him if you don't want to marry him?" Now Aiden had joined them, causing Lou to pause and look at her older son.

Might as well make it a family party.

"Yeah. Isn't that the whole purpose of dating—finding someone who could be a husband?" Emma questioned.

Her parenting victory had been short lived.

"Or wife," Cash clarified as Aiden shuddered. The idea of ever having a wife was too much for his nine-year-old brain.

"That's one reason to go on a date," Lou said as she went into her closet to change, thankful for the refuge from the barrage of questions. There were a whole lot of reasons to date that Lou wasn't about to share with young ears. Her reason for going out with Preston's dad was a little more G-rated—giving herself dating experience. But even that felt a little too mature of a reason to tell her kids. Especially if it led to a conversation about why she wanted experience.

"What are the other reasons?" Aiden asked through the closet door. Probably wondering if he'd ever have to go on a date.

Other reasons to date. Lou just had to come up with one. One reason to date that she could tell her kids. She frantically brainstormed ideas as she adjusted the yellow top and emerged from the closet, keeping her eyes on the mirror rather than her four too-inquisitive children.

"Um, it's a way grownups enjoy spending time together," Lou said. There, one! She'd done it. It was a little lame but was all she could come up with at the moment.

"Why do grownups want to spend time together?" Hazel cocked her head the other direction.

Excellent question. Lou wished there was someone else who would answer . . . she wanted to know, too.

"It's like when you go spend time with your friends," she finally explained.

"Oh. So you want to be Preston's dad's friend," Aiden said, nodding as if that made much more sense.

"Yes!" Thank you, Aiden. That was exactly right. Well, maybe not exactly. It was more like Lou was going out with him because he'd actually asked her out and she really should be dating again. Did that mean she was using Preston's dad? She hoped not. But not going out with him would have been worse, right? And why did she keep calling the man 'Preston's dad'? She knew full well it was C.J. . . . drat, was it J.C.?

"Can I wear lipstick when I go to Mabel's house?" Hazel asked hopefully.

"No," Lou and Emma said in unison. Count on Emma to follow the rules.

"But you're putting on lipstick to see your friend," Hazel countered.

And this was why dating should happen before one had children.

Lou turned from the mirror to see Emma glaring at Hazel for even deigning to ask such a question. Meanwhile Hazel was oblivious, Aiden looked as if he'd just been forced to eat a cucumber (his least favorite food), and Cash was grinning.

Thankfully Hazel seemed to have forgotten her opposition to Lou wearing lipstick when she couldn't.

"You look pretty, Mom," Cash approved.

"Thanks, Cash." Lou ruffled his hair and then Aiden's. Hazel held up her arms and Lou picked her up. With how big she was getting Lou wasn't sure how much longer she'd get these kinds of hugs, so she savored them while she could.

The doorbell rang. Alexis was here, and that meant their conversation was over. She breathed a sigh of pure relief. Doubtless some version of it would happen again, but Lou would take the reprieve even for a short time.

"You four be good for Alexis, got it?" Lou said, throwing the "mom look" at them as she hurried toward the front door.

Alexis was an angel. She'd offered to babysit before Lou could even ask.

"What do you mean by good?" Aiden asked cautiously, following behind his mom with the rest of his siblings.

"You know what I mean. And so does Alexis."

Thankfully Alexis had plenty of Aiden experience.

"And what if we aren't good . . . hypothetically?" Aiden asked.

Lou wished she knew who'd taught him that word. He used it at the most inopportune times.

"Hypothetically? You'd be grounded and lose your allowance for at least two weeks," Lou replied as she turned to her son.

All questions vanished from Aiden's face. Thank heavens.

"Mom, can we go with you? If you're going to play with your friend?" Hazel asked as Lou opened the door for Alexis.

Alexis began laughing.

"That's what you're calling it?" she asked between giggles.

"Shut it," Lou said to her friend before turning to Hazel.

"No, baby girl. You can't come." She dropped to her

haunches so that she was eye level with Hazel. "But we'll do something fun soon."

"Me too?" Cash asked.

"Shut it," Hazel said to her brother before Lou could respond.

"We don't say 'shut it,'" Emma reprimanded her sister.

"Mom just did," Hazel responded.

"No one should say that. I'm sorry," Lou said, grabbing her purse and looking at a still grinning Alexis.

Lou glared in her best friend's direction. She needed backup and Alexis just viewed her as entertainment.

Lou huffed, causing Alexis to double over. Lou pinched her lips. Who would be laughing after a few hours with her kids?

C.J. TOOK one last gulp of his diet root beer—well, Lou's diet root beer that C.J. had insisted she order. One that Lou knew she didn't want because she hadn't been able to stomach root beer since her third pregnancy, but C.J. had told her to go all out. It was on him. And then he'd ordered for her.

Lou tried to feel grateful. It was nice that the man was taking her out and insisted on paying. She was getting a free meal and really shouldn't be complaining. The diner was fine. Granted, the only people on dates around them were under the age of eighteen, but you know, it was different . . . fine.

And it would have felt more fine if what had happened before the diet root beer incident hadn't already rubbed Lou the wrong way. When they'd first gotten to the diner Lou had been wavering between the guac burger and the chicken sandwich. As she debated, C.J. had suggested the chicken Caesar salad. Lou wasn't a huge Caesar dressing fan, but as she opened her mouth to tell C.J. that, their waitress had come by to take their order. C.J. had given his and then proceeded to order for Lou. A chicken Caesar salad with the dressing on the side, as well as a side of fries.

Lou should have said something. She would have said something, but she'd been flabbergasted. She'd never had a man order for her. Especially something she didn't want. But she'd chalked it up to C.J. being a little overzealous.

So after she'd picked at her salad and inhaled her fries, she'd been starving and was more than ready for dessert. And Lou wanted nothing more than a butterscotch sundae. But C.J. had taken over again, insisting that the diet root beer was amazing, almost like a real dessert. This time Lou had been prepared, politely but clearly stating that she didn't want the diet root beer. But C.J. had interrupted once more, telling her she was adorable. She was still trying to process the weird compliment when he told her to go all out as he was paying. Minutes later Lou was staring at a diet root beer she couldn't drink.

And now they were here. Finally at the end of this interminable date.

Lou was practically chomping at the bit to escape. She was so grateful she'd driven herself and was already planning her order at a drive-through on the way home. At least she could chalk this date up to a good story to tell Alexis.

"You said you didn't have plans after this, didn't you?" C.J. asked, interrupting Lou's fantasy of her great escape.

Lou felt the urge to throttle her past self. Why the heck had she told him that? She'd just been thrown off when he'd asked that as the first sentence of their date. He'd literally said, "Hey, you look great. Do you have any plans after this?"

Lou had assumed he was wondering if she had dressed up for some other event after the date. She'd wanted to assure him that she was taking their date seriously, but now she wished she'd lied. Said anything besides that she was free as a bird all evening.

She thought about lying now, saying one of her kids wasn't feeling well, but with her luck C.J. would insist on going home with her and she'd probably do something stupid like say her child had some highly contagious plague and before Lou knew it the CDC as well as CPS would be at her door.

So Lou said the only thing she could. "Yeah, I did."

She worked hard not to cringe. At least outwardly. Inwardly she was cringing up a storm.

"Awesome. I already have our movie tickets. The show starts in twenty minutes." C.J. was all smiles, as if this was the best date he'd ever been on.

Surely Lou wasn't reading him right. He couldn't think that this date was going well, could he? He had to at least feel there was no chemistry between the two of them, right? She'd called him Preston's dad more than once. To his face.

"Yay." Lou tried to find some enthusiasm.

"I could drive you to the theater," C.J. pressed.

He'd been trying to drive Lou all night but she wanted her car around, just in case. And as nice as it was to have an out, her problem was that she wasn't able to access her out.

But maybe she would soon?

A girl could hope.

"That's okay. I'm kind of a control freak and like to be the one behind the wheel," Lou said. It was kind of the truth. She was a control freak. But she had let Harvey drive for most of their marriage.

"I like it," C.J. said with a grin. "That's okay, I'll just ride with you."

Lou was so stunned she had no idea how her face must look. Did she look disgusted or horrified . . . or was she simply gaping like a fish?

"Um." How in the heck was she supposed to get out of this?

"The movie will probably be ending late and I really should let you get home to Preston," Lou finally managed. She turned on her heel and booked it out of the restaurant before she or C.J. could say anything else. She didn't slow until she got in her car.

She paused for a moment before realizing she wouldn't put it past C.J. to just show up in her car so she'd better get going.

She peeled out of the parking lot and headed for the theater.

Why on earth was she driving to the theater? She really wanted to leave this date. But how? She was halfway tempted to turn around and go home. No, that wasn't kind. If Emma or Hazel were in this situation Lou would hope they'd stick it out. Finish the date or at least have the class to tell the guy it was over. At least Lou would get a bit more dating experience under her belt. Yeah, that was her silver lining in all of this. And she'd cling to that for the remainder of this awful date.

Lou made it to the theater in record time, pulled into a parking spot, and stopped the car. She leaned her forehead on the steering wheel and started to take a breath, a moment to herself, when C.J.'s car pulled up beside hers.

Oh please no.

She wanted to close her eyes and will the whole situation away but C.J. knocked on her window.

"You okay in there?" he called. "I could join you if you need some company."

That was all the motivation Lou needed to unclip her seatbelt and practically leap out of the car.

"I'm good." She made a desperate attempt at a smile. Why was it so hard to smile?

It was only then that she realized she didn't even know what movie they'd be seeing. Not that it really mattered. As long as she had a huge tub of popcorn and it was loud enough to keep her from needing to carry a conversation, it sounded perfect.

Not that the conversation at the diner had been all bad. Lou had enjoyed learning more about Preston. But it seemed every story ended up being about C.J.'s ex, even stories that Lou had started. C.J. would take over and somehow they'd wind up talking about his ex again. She seemed like a lovely woman.

Lou had found out during their conversation that his ex was an incredible kisser and cuddler, that she'd had a hard time making friends when she'd moved to Seattle at fourteen, and that Caesar salad was her favorite food.

All of it was weird and way more than Lou wanted to know about the woman she'd never met but the last detail was more than a little creepy, considering how C.J. had forced her to eat the same, but whatever.

"I'll get popcorn since you got our meal and the tickets," Lou offered as they walked into the theater, the smell of butter cheering her up immediately.

"Oh, I'm not sure about popcorn. After all we ate. You did get the *fries*. Are you sure that's a good idea?" C.J.'s eyes drifted down to Lou's stomach as he spoke and she narrowly resisted the urge to smack him.

Instead she smiled and said, "It sounds lovely to me," before marching her all too thick stomach to the candy counter and buying herself a large popcorn as well as a box of candy and a giant Coke. No diet or zero for her; she wanted every drop of sugar in that thing.

C.J. stood to the side, watching her every move and surely judging her, but Lou was done with best date behavior. She was barely holding onto civil human behavior.

"Do you have any idea how much sugar is in that?" C.J. commented after Lou had joined him and they began to walk toward the screen where their movie was showing.

Lou pumped her eyebrows. Because what was she supposed to say to that?

When they got to the door of their theater, Lou looked up at the marquee above it and her feet slowed to a stop.

"Halloween Horror Nights?" Her voice faltered a bit.

She'd heard of the movie—it was practically every other commercial on TV now that they'd entered October—but had zero desire to watch it. Heck, she turned away from the commercial every time, she hated the idea of the movie so much.

Lou began shaking her head.

"I get it. My ex hated horror movies too. But then she'd jump on me and she was such a good cuddler, you know."

Lou just kept shaking her head. No, she couldn't do this anymore. His ex again? This was all too weird and horrible and . . . she just wanted to go home.

But she couldn't just leave him, could she? Wasn't that rude?

Maybe if they watched a different movie.

"I can't do it, C.J. I really hate horror movies. I'll buy us tickets to another movie. Any other movie. Just not this one." Lou was nearly pleading but she wouldn't survive this movie. Especially if C.J. hoped there would be cuddling.

C.J. sighed, his gaze filled with dissatisfaction, all of which was directed toward Lou. "I don't think that's necessary. I'm just . . . I've got to say I'm a little disappointed. I'd hoped this date would go much better." He took a step back, his intent clear.

You and me both, buddy, thought Lou but kept her mouth shut. Because as humiliating as it was to be dumped in the middle of a date—people were stopping to watch the preshow she and C.J. were providing—finishing the date would be worse. If Lou said something and inadvertently made him change his mind, she would never forgive herself.

"I mean, I planned this nice night and not only do you try to order a burger when we both know the salad was the better choice for you—"

Lou literally bit her lip to keep from speaking. Behind C.J., she saw a woman's mouth drop open.

"You say you don't like root beer but then you order all of this junk," C.J. continued, waving a hand over her snacks in disgust.

Lou wasn't sure what her dislike of root beer had to do with anything, but okay.

"You're just nothing like her," he finished.

Lou's stomach churned. Her. She knew exactly who C.J. was referring to. Had he been trying to replace his ex with Lou? Find some woman to fill the exact spot she'd left behind?

Lou wanted to scrub her arms; just the thought of it made her feel so icky. There were so many things wrong with what C.J. had said that Lou didn't even know where to start.

"I think it's better we go our separate ways now. I hope this won't make soccer games awkward." C.J. looked at Lou pityingly, as if she would break with this revelation.

He couldn't be that clueless to her feelings, could he? And holy Hannah, soccer games would be awkward, but not for the reason C.J. thought.

"I understand," Lou finally said, snapping her mouth closed again. She wanted to add more to her answer, something along the lines of *hallelujah*, especially for their growing audience. To let them all know that C.J. was doing her a huge favor and that she'd been trying to leave their date for the last two hours, but she kept silent. She was worried that anything she might say would either sound cruel or ridiculous. It was better to leave things alone. Who cared if people thought C.J. dumped her in the middle of their first date? The only people who would relish in her failure would be Felicity, Harvey's new girlfriend, and her friends. And Lou had come to a place where she couldn't care a rat's behind about any of their opinions.

"Good," C.J. said. He took a careful step toward her, reached awkwardly around her and patted Lou's back.

Yes, he actually patted her back. Alexis was going to love that little bright spot of the night.

"We can be friends." C.J. offered an olive branch.

Lou took that as him trying. Yes, he was clueless and really hung up on his ex and a little bit rude but Lou would try to look past all of that.

"Sure," she said with a slight nod.

"Awesome," C.J. said with a grin.

Finally, they were done. This date from H-E-double hockey sticks was over. Lou smiled as well, genuinely this time.

C.J. looked like he was going to turn around and leave when he added, "Oh, and as your friend, maybe ease up on the treats."

C.J. walked away and Lou resisted the primal urge to throw said treats at his retreating form. She was above that.

Besides, if she did she wouldn't have snacks for the long, long story she'd be telling Alexis when she got home. They were going to need every bit of this popcorn.

CHAPTER EIGHT

"SORRY I'M A LITTLE LATE TODAY," Piper said as she seated herself on the grass next to a headstone she wished didn't have to exist.

"I know you're going to say that I shouldn't have come at all. That these daily visits aren't healthy. I need to spend more time talking to the living than the dead." Piper choked up on that last word.

This wasn't the way of the world. She shouldn't have to visit her daughter's grave. Yet here she stood. A mother, visiting her daughter in the cemetery.

Her heart constricted.

No. Piper took a breath and tried to push all negative emotion away. This wasn't what Kristie would want. She wouldn't want her mother to feel pain at every thought of her. She'd want these moments with Piper on this beautiful hillside to be the bright spot of her day. Kristie would never want her memory to bring Piper down, only to lift. The way she always had in life.

"I saw Brock this morning. On Main Street," Piper said

softly, knowing she didn't need to speak over the wind. Kristie would hear her regardless.

"I know you know. I imagined you walking beside me. I'm sure you were watching from heaven," Piper continued as she saw the scene play out in her mind.

She'd been on her way to the bank, passing the coffee shop. Brock should have been in school, but maybe it was a school holiday? Piper didn't know these things anymore. But he'd been hand in hand with a girl. A cute girl, just as Kristie would have wanted for him.

But he'd dropped the girl's hand like it was a hot brick and his cheeks had flamed red when he made eye contact with Piper.

Piper didn't want it to be that way. Kristie wouldn't have wanted it either. She would have wanted the boy she loved to move on, to find his happiness with a sweet girl, the way it looked like he had.

But guilt had filled his features, so Piper felt the need to say something when Brock came out of the coffee shop alone to speak to Piper.

"She'd be thrilled," Piper had said.

Brock had shaken his head, gaze on his shoes. "No. She could have only been thrilled for me if she was alive. And if she were here, I wouldn't even be looking at another girl."

Piper's eyes had welled with tears. She understood. Wanting to honor who Kristie had been yet feeling it was so wrong because she should have been there. She should have been the one holding Brock's hand, lifting the other in greeting when she saw her mom pass.

"I miss her so much." Brock's voice had broken as he finally lifted his eyes and Piper saw into their hurt, conflicted depths.

The tears had flowed down Piper's cheeks. "Me too," she had whispered. "Get back in there, Brock."

"It doesn't feel right," he had managed through heavy breaths.

"One day it will." Piper had made a promise she didn't know if she could keep. But it had felt necessary.

Brock had nodded once and then opened the door to the coffee shop.

Piper had left before he could look back. He didn't need any more reminders of the way it had been. He was a young man with so much life ahead of him. He deserved to see a bright future.

"But I'm sure you're wondering what I thought. You always wanted to know what I thought about things. It made me feel so important. You made me feel important."

Piper bit her lip. Feeling like she had lost her role as a mother had been one of the biggest blows to losing Kristie. Although she knew she'd be a mother forever, she was no longer as needed, as adored, as guilelessly loved.

"Anyway . . . " Piper said when her thoughts became too deep. She knew Kristie would have laughed.

"I'm happy for him. It's been over half a year."

She paused. "Wow, has it really been that long?"

Seven months and four days to be exact. Seven months and four days since Piper last saw her daughter's beautiful eyes. Seven months and four days since she last heard her say 'I love you.' Seven months and four days since she last held Kristie in her arms, since she last got to mother the most wonderful girl on the planet.

"He was smiling before he realized I was there. She makes him smile. You want that, right?"

Piper put on her sunglasses and lay down on the grass next to Kristie's grave. It was cloudy, not a single ray shining, but she still didn't want to stare up at where the sun should be without eye protection.

"I know you do."

Piper paused, thinking about the other part of her morning.

"Seren called. She is a force of nature, let me tell you. She wants me to join her at some fundraiser in LA next month. We'll schmooze. I told you about her golden face comment, right? She is a hoot. Anyway, I guess I'm going and as much as it thrills me to be helping other teens, part of me aches that you'll never get to see this new teen hangout. I know you would have loved it. But I'm trying to concentrate on the good this will do. Use it to make me smile more. I know you want me to smile more. He makes me smile."

Piper had moved from Brock to Seren and now to Carter. She didn't think Kristie would mind.

"Can you believe he's still here?" Piper asked, crossing one foot over the other. "I thought he would leave the island right after your funeral. But he's still around.

"He said he wants to be my husband again. Did you cheer when he told me how he felt? You would have if you were in that room. Carter had no bigger fan, even with the millions out there in the world, than you.

"He's the only one that makes me feel anything like me again. I thought it would be impossible, in those first couple of months I could barely breathe, let alone feel. But I am again. I'm feeling lots of things, Kristie. And it scares me."

Piper felt a little dizzy from lying flat on her back. She sat up, scooting back until she was leaning against Kristie's headstone.

"Is this weird?" Piper asked. "Me using your headstone as a backrest? It's strange how I can go from so morose to feeling perfectly at home in this place. It's probably because I know part of you is here. Anywhere you are is home."

"Oh Kristie." Piper let the tears fall.

She pulled off her sunglasses and stuck them back in her

bag. Now that she wasn't staring up at the sky there was no need for them, even though it was midday. The gray sky matched Piper's tumultuous feelings.

After a few minutes of crying, Piper was done. She was sure Kristie felt sick of it. So she dried her eyes.

"I know you're dying for me to get back to what I was talking about. I never tell you what I'm feeling about your dad. In life it felt like too much for you to bear. But now, I think you'd want to know. And if you don't want to hear it, go hide away in some corner of heaven where you can't hear me."

Piper smiled, imagining Kristie covering her ears and yelling, "TMI, Mom!"

"I love being held by him. There is nothing better in the world. And I really, really want to kiss him."

She imagined the groan that confession would illicit.

"Don't pretend that kissing Brock wasn't one of your favorite things in the world. I feel the same way about kissing your dad."

Piper grinned as she considered finally giving in to her craving.

"But I'm scared, Kristie. If I push past this physical and emotional boundary I've set up to keep myself protected, what happens if he leaves again?"

Piper drew in a deep breath. "I know he's changed. A lot. You don't have to tell me every way that he has. I've seen it. He's not that same man who left us years ago. I'm not the same woman either."

"I can't let him leave," Piper finally voiced her number one truth. "But if I ask him to stay I have to give myself to him. It would be so easy. A few words. And yet I don't know if I can. Because if I tell him what I'm feeling we'll be together, and things will move so fast. We don't need to date because we already know everything about each other. And not even just our old selves who were married. I know no one better than Carter right at this moment and I know it's the same for him. We've been so intertwined in the other's life these past couple years since he's been back on the island. I know every part of him and he knows each scar of mine. And he still loves me, Kristie."

Carter loved her. And she loved Carter. She knew if she told him to leave the island it would be her biggest mistake, an eternal regret.

But did she have the courage to let her guard down, to allow Carter into the deepest parts of her?

Then again, hadn't he already been there? In those moments when she'd been too broken to do anything other than exist, when the walls had been down. And Carter had been there.

If Piper really thought about it, there was literally nothing keeping them apart now. No worry of Kristie becoming attached and then hurt if things didn't work out. And if Piper was honest with herself, she was pretty sure things would work out. Carter had proved he would put in whatever amount of toil and effort was necessary to make that happen. Piper would too.

She loved Carter and he loved her. They were both willing to make this relationship work. They were more than ready for the next step . . . in some ways they'd already passed the next step. Piper didn't need to decide to take it; she just needed to realize they were already there.

"Are you calling me an idiot?" Piper asked aloud. "Because I am. Why did it take me so long to see this? It's not about figuring out if I love him. I've always loved him. And he's proved his love over and over. I've wasted so much time I could have been kissing Carter."

Piper laughed at that last line even though it was the truth.

"So what now?" Piper asked.

Tell him.

Piper didn't know if the words came from her own mind but she knew they were said in Kristie's voice.

And when she looked up to the sky to thank her daughter, she saw a single ray of light shining down through the cloudy skies, landing on the trees that divided the road from the cemetery. As Piper's eyes followed the ray down, out of the trees came Carter.

She bit her lip before asking in her mind, "Did you bring him?"

Kristie's laugh filled her ears . . . and then it was gone.

"I saw your car parked and thought I'd join you. Is that alright, or do you want to be alone?" Carter called out as he approached.

Piper shook her head, not sure words would come right then. She knew others could explain away what she'd heard and felt. She was a grieving mother, surely hoping to hear her child's voice and laughter. But for Piper it had all been too real to brush off as her own mind. Kristie had been there, urging Piper to the one person who would be the most help for her in her journey of healing. The person Kristie had pushed Piper toward during life as well.

Carter set the single lily he'd brought on a grave nearby before tucking his long legs under him and sitting on the ground next to Piper.

Because of how often Piper and Carter visited Kristie's grave, the number of flowers and other offerings they brought had become overwhelming for the one grave. They'd considered stopping but then Carter had noticed all of the empty gravesites around Kristie's. He'd suggested that they keep bringing things but instead leave them on those other graves. Piper had loved the idea and it had now become somewhat of a tradition. No one went without flowers. They tried to remember each person there. Everyone deserved their memory to be kept alive, even in this small way.

Carter brought his hand close to Piper's face. "May I?" he asked.

Piper wasn't sure what he was asking but she nodded again.

His thumb gently rubbed under her eye as his fingers cradled the back of her head. His face moved closer to inspect what he was doing.

Piper closed her eyes, relishing Carter's touch. More than needing this, she realized she wanted this. And so much more.

She opened her eyes to see Carter watching her.

"Were you crying?" Carter asked, his breath warm on her cheek.

Piper felt her belly warm and lips tingle.

Maybe you should stop wasting time, Mom. So you can get to the kissing.

Piper grinned before remembering Carter had asked a question.

Crying. Right. "Aren't I always?" she tried to joke.

"Not always. But too much. I wish I could take the pain for you," Carter said sincerely. Piper knew it was the truth. Even with how much he had to be feeling, reeling from the death of their daughter, he was still willing to take on all of her pain as well.

If she couldn't trust a man like that, she'd trust no one ever. And Piper wanted to trust again. To give her heart and receive Carter's in return.

Piper's eyes dropped to Carter's lips, and the urge to press hers against his was overwhelming. But not yet. Words had to be said. They needed to come to an understanding. She wanted their kiss to mean more than her taking from him in her time of need, something she'd been doing far too often these past couple of years.

"So I've been talking to Kristie," Piper said.

She loved that Carter just smiled, his left dimple showing. Most would probably look at her with concern or maybe pity. But Carter knew she did this all the time, understood her need to feel a connection to their daughter. She was pretty sure he sometimes came to talk to her too.

"She's a good listener," he said simply, his gentle smile growing.

"The best. And I . . . well, I was talking to her about us," Piper said, her cheeks warming. It was an intimate revelation.

But Carter just watched Piper, proving he was a good listener as well.

"I was telling her how good you've been to me, even though I'm sure she already knew," Piper said.

She knew if Kristie was allowed any time back with them she would surely be present in the moments when her parents were making their way back toward one another. It had been her greatest wish. And as much as Piper wanted to do right by her daughter, she knew she couldn't go back to Carter just because it was what Kristie would have wanted for them. But now she was sure. Her decision did factor in what Kristie had hoped for her, because Kristie loved her, and she'd also considered who Carter was now, who she was now, her feelings, Carter's feelings. It had taken her maybe a bit too long but she'd finally realized the truth.

"I hope she's seeing that," Carter said before opening his arms.

Piper scooted right into them, settling her back against his chest. This would be much easier to say without looking Carter in the eye. She wasn't sure why she was so nervous, but she was. Her heart beat hard against her ribcage.

She'd be done soon.

"I think one of my biggest fears was that I can't love you the way that I did," Piper began.

"Oh," was all Carter said.

It wasn't until he responded with that single syllable that Piper realized how bad that could sound and decided she needed to hurry through the rest of her speech.

"You can't love me the way you did either. We've been through too much to go back to that."

"Oh," Carter said again but this time there was a lightness, an understanding, in his voice.

Good.

"But if I didn't love you in that way, how was I supposed to make this work? I didn't understand how we, as the same two people, could find a brand new kind of love, even after we'd changed so much. But Kristie helped me to see we've already found that new love. I just had to see it."

Piper felt Carter nod.

"My fears that I couldn't replicate what we had were so silly. Why did I want that when it had failed? What we needed this time around was to learn and to grow and to relearn to love one another in a better way."

Carter nodded again.

"I needed to grieve. To let my heart mourn. To know that moving on in my life didn't mean leaving Kristie behind. I needed to see your gentle kindness with me. Basically what I'm trying to say is that we had to go through all that we went through to get here. So why was I trying to go back a thousand steps? I used so many things as a shield: my grief, my fear, our past, all of it. But no more."

Piper heard Carter suck in a breath.

"I'm done being scared, Carter. I'm done pushing you away. I'm done taking and never giving. I want to be the woman you need. The woman you want."

"Done and done," Carter said as he leaned down to speak into Piper's ear.

She ignored the fluttering in her chest. A few more words first.

"I love you, Carter. I choose you, I want you, and I need you," Piper said as she turned in Carter's arms.

There, she'd told him. She was in the right frame of mind; she was ready. For him. For them. For their future.

"And I love you, Piper," Carter said earnestly, his eyes full of hope and yearning. "I haven't always been the man I should have been, the man you deserved, but I promise you from this moment on, I'll do my best to be that man. I know I'll stumble—"

"And I'll be there to pick you up," Piper promised.

"But I'll never stop trying. I'll never give up."

Piper nodded. She could promise the same. It wouldn't be easy, and it wouldn't be perfect. They were too experienced in love and life to think differently. But it would be theirs. It would be forged from their sorrows and lifted with their hopes. Beautiful in its imperfections.

"So are we dating now?" Piper asked. It didn't seem an adequate relationship term for what she felt for Carter, for what was between them now.

"More than that, right?" Carter asked, searching her eyes. He obviously wanted to plunge forward but was making sure Piper wanted to jump as well.

Piper nodded as she reached into her purse and pulled out a ring she'd carried with her ever since Kristie had been given her terminal diagnosis. It had been Piper's stability even when she didn't know what it had meant to her. It had been a symbol of her and Carter. Of what they'd had. Of what she'd hoped they'd one day have again even before she was willing to think those thoughts.

"I thought you got rid of this thing," Carter said as he took the ring that Piper offered, turning the symbol of their first marriage in his hand. "I should get you a new one."

The gold band held a single emerald.

They'd been too poor for a real ring when they'd first married and Carter had given Piper a silver band, promising her more one day. On their third anniversary, after they'd had Kristie, Carter had upgraded to this ring. They were still too poor for a diamond but the emerald, Kristie's birthstone, had meant so much more to Piper than a traditional ring.

Piper shook her head. "It's her way of still being here." Piper didn't need to tell Carter who 'her' was.

Carter nodded. Kristie had often said she wanted a ring just like this one when she got married.

Carter stood, pulling Piper to her feet before dropping to one knee, the ring that meant so much to both of them in his hand. The symbol of what they'd had, blossoming into what they'd grown into, would now also be a symbol of what they'd strive for.

"Piper, you deserve the world. The first time I did this I made promises of forever that I failed to keep. Please let me make that up to you. Let me be the man you thought I could be. And let me be the man who will walk with you not just through the trials of life but also during every blissful moment. Will you be my wife?" Carter asked as he looked up at Piper.

"Again?" Piper couldn't help but tease.

"For the final time," Carter replied. He smiled at her joke, but she could see that he meant every word with all his heart.

Piper nodded as Carter slipped their ring onto her finger. The ghost of where that ring should have been had always haunted Piper. Now it felt right. Maybe not quite complete—nothing would ever be again without Kristie—but somehow at the same time whole. No longer broken.

Carter stood and wrapped one arm around Piper's waist, pulling her close as he stroked her cheek with his free hand.

"I never thought I'd have you in my arms like this again," Carter said with reverence.

Piper understood. And she was loving the words, but she also wanted to get to the kissing.

"Are you just going to stand there and look at me?" she teased with a grin.

Carter chuckled before closing the distance between them, finally meeting her lips. Piper flung her arms over Carter's shoulders, winding her fingers through his hair and pulling him even closer.

And that was how Carter and Piper became engaged once more. In the cemetery. Some might say it was a morbid place to restart their lives together but for Piper and Carter it was just as it should be. Even if Kristie was surely somewhere in heaven laughing at her parents.

CHAPTER NINE

"HOW ARE YOU HOLDING UP?" Wendy asked as she quietly entered Julia's home after her shift at the bank.

"Uh, yeah," Julia said softly even though there was no way her mom and sister could hear her. They were both resting in their respective rooms, exhausted from the day of travel.

"Already?" Wendy asked as she eyed the stairs uncertainly, as if she weren't sure whether she wanted to go up and see the family who had come to visit her.

"Well, according to Mom the flight was too long, the ferry ride too short, cars here make too much noise, and the air smells like salt."

Wendy winced.

"And according to your mom the airport was too busy, the ferry workers thought too much of themselves, and everything feels sticky. Why did we have to move to a place that has the ocean?"

Wendy sighed before shaking her head. "Sounds like you can take the women out of Travers but it does nothing to change their behavior." She said the words in a joking manner, and she absolutely did love both her mother and grandmother, but the message was still true. Julia's mom and sister were determined to see the world through a lens hazy with their displeasures.

"You'd think the first class flight you bought them would have been something to be grateful for," Wendy added optimistically. Probably hoping that Julia had forgotten about her mom and grandma "praising" the flight.

"The cabin was too cold and the aisles were too narrow. Why would they waste so much room on the seats when they were plenty big but not leave any room for a woman to walk through?" Julia mimicked her mom with the last words.

Julia saw the defeat in Wendy's eyes and felt badly. She'd been wanting to commiserate with someone who understood, but that wasn't fair. Yes, she'd had an unfortunate afternoon full of complaining but she didn't have to bring Wendy down with her.

"I'm sure they're just tired. They've been resting for a few hours and now that their favorite person is here, all will be well," Julia said.

Wendy gave a short laugh as she shook her head. "Don't try to sugarcoat it for me, Aunt Julia. It's better for me to be reminded now how it's going to be instead of hoping for the best and being served the worst."

"Now who's a Debbie Downer?" Julia teased.

Wendy laughed, this time for real.

"Why does this danged house have to have so many rooms? No one should get lost in their own home." Betty Price's voice carried clearly down the stairs, tinged with annoyance. Apparently she'd made it out of the guest room she was staying in and was practically to the stairs. She wasn't as lost as she wanted everyone to think she was.

"At least you got a room with an ocean view. My windows overlook the driveway." Lacey's disapproving voice joined her mother's.

Julia had put Lacey in a garden-facing guest room. The very edge of the driveway was visible from the windows but mostly the view was the lush green grass that was still beautiful in the fall and dense, pretty bushes surrounding the property. A room Julia had chosen for her because she'd been complaining about the stickiness on the island. Julia figured her sister wouldn't want to see the cause of the humidity that was driving her crazy. Of course, as always, Julia's decision was wrong.

"Ready or not," Wendy muttered before she started up the wide, dark wood staircase that Lacey had called overly large and kind of obnoxious.

"Hi Mom, Grandma!" Wendy called ahead.

"Wendy?" Betty asked.

"Are you finally home from work? I mean, most daughters would take the day off if they heard their mom and grandma were coming into town, but I guess you have good work ethics?" Lacey disguised the barb as a question.

Only eight days to go, Julia told herself.

Two days after Ellis had left for Nashville, Julia had gotten the call. Her mom and sister could be there in three days. There had been a flurry of reservations and getting the house ready for guests, but Julia, with the help of her cleaning staff, had done it.

Getting first class nonstop tickets with so little time to spare had been a bit of an issue but Julia's travel agent had worked a miracle. Although to hear it from Betty, the inconvenience of flying out of St. Louis instead of Springfield had been almost too much to bear. Even though the difference in their drive time to the airport was literally ten minutes since Travers was between the two cities.

The last-minute nature of the trip was also why Wendy hadn't been able to get the day off. Her boss had done her a huge favor by granting vacation time for several of the days her mom and grandma were in town but they'd needed her to come in today.

Apparently Wendy's best wasn't good enough for Lacey.

Nope. Julia couldn't start thinking like that already. They would never survive this visit if Julia didn't try to keep her thoughts more charitable.

"Good to see you, Mom," Wendy said as she gave Lacey a hug and then moved to Betty.

The two women seemed no more refreshed than they'd looked when Julia had left them in their rooms a couple of hours before. That didn't bode well for the rest of the evening.

"How is it only six pm?" Lacey asked as she looked at her watch and then started down the stairs.

"It feels like it should be eight," Betty said, following her daughter.

"That's because in Travers it is eight," Wendy said, before biting her lip. Surely biting back a laugh.

Julia needed to do the same—to find humor instead of insult.

"You all have to have your fancy island time," Betty grumbled.

Yes, Julia was sorry Pacific standard time was such an inconvenience for her family.

Ah! She needed to stop it. But at least thinking the snide remarks rather than saying them was an improvement for her.

The doorbell rang and Julia almost shouted for joy. Thank goodness for meal deliveries.

"And that should be dinner," she said in her most cheerful voice as she went to the door. The others had joined her in the foyer.

"Couldn't be bothered to cook on the first night her mom and sister came into town," Lacey muttered.

Julia felt her feathers ruffle before she reminded herself that it was the truth. She truly hadn't bothered to cook. Not when she knew she'd be exhausted from dealing with her family.

"Yes! Moon Garden," Wendy said delightedly. "They have the best Thai food I've ever had."

Lacey crinkled her nose.

"I hate curry," Betty said as she eyed the bags.

"Good thing I got noodles, stir fry chicken, and appetizers as well," Julia said as she lifted the bags.

"Hm," Betty said, probably reserving judgment.

Which Julia would take.

She led them all into her kitchen, passing the formal dining room on the way.

"Is this room too fancy for us?" Lacey asked, raising her eyebrows as they walked past.

"Nope. We can eat there if you'd like. I just usually choose to use the breakfast nook for family gatherings," Julia said as she stopped so that her mom and sister could decide where to eat.

"All those family gatherings you're having without us?" Lacey looked from her sister to her daughter.

Wendy was biting her lip once more but this time it didn't look like she was holding back laughter.

"Why do you have two eating tables? You just need the one," Betty muttered.

Julia prayed for patience.

"I think the breakfast nook will be perfect, Aunt Julia," Wendy declared. She started toward it at a brisk walk, the rest of the group trailing after her.

"Breakfast nook. What a silly name," Betty said as if Julia had invented the term herself.

Julia looked at the clock. Six oh five. She'd made it five minutes with her mom and sister and she was ready to run from the house screaming.

Julia began unloading the bags as Wendy gathered plates and cutlery.

"That's so nice that you know your way around your aunt's home," Lacey said.

Julia smiled. Was that an actual compliment? She could do this.

"Although I'm guessing you've forgotten these same things about our house since you decided to leave us and move here," Lacey added.

Wendy's eyes shot flames before she looked down to the ground. Julia did the same. Maybe she couldn't do this.

But she had to. For Wendy's sake . . . and for her own. She wanted family, even if it was this one.

Julia opened the boxes of takeout as Wendy passed out the plates.

"Help yourself," Julia offered as she sat and motioned for her mom and sister to go first.

"She has this whole, huge house and yet there's no one here to help with the meals. Didn't think we'd have to serve ourselves in this fancy place," Betty said, just loudly enough for all of them to hear.

Julia pinched her leg hard. She hoped that would keep her mouth shut. She wasn't sure how but she'd used up every other way of keeping her patience.

"Keep the curry far from me," Betty added in a louder voice when Lacey took the Panang curry as her first portion.

"I wasn't bringing it anywhere near you, Ma," Lacey said in a tone Julia wished she could use with her mother. But Betty would freak the flip out if Julia ever spoke like that.

"Aunt Julia?" Wendy offered Julia the container of drunken noodles she'd just served herself.

"Thanks, Hon," Julia said, taking the box and filling her

plate. Maybe this was like a marathon. Get enough carbs in her and she'd survive.

"Oh cute. They have little nicknames for each other," Lacey said to her mom, her lip curling.

"That's it!" Wendy's neck muscles strained as she yelled, startling everyone at the table. Betty dropped her spoon at the sudden noise but Julia and Lacey just jumped before turning wide eyes on Wendy.

"You two are getting a beautiful island getaway. Away from the stresses of life in a gorgeous home that we could have only dreamed of vacationing at in if it weren't for Aunt Julia's generosity."

"We're family, Wendy. This is what family does. Or did living in this place make you forget that?" Lacey countered quickly.

"The only thing I forgot while I was here was how incredibly difficult you and Grandma can make things. Why can't you just say thank you? Why can't you acknowledge that you two decided to come last minute and that like any normal job it was hard for me to get time off with so little notice? Why can't you see the beauty in the ocean and the lush green landscape? Why can't you take a minute to think about anyone other than your own spoiled selves?!"

Lacey turned to Julia. "Is this how you taught her to treat her mother?"

"This isn't about her! It's about you! You know I said this kind of stuff to you back in Travers so don't you dare blame it on Aunt Julia. She's been nothing but a support to me. She put her life on the back burner to make sure I'm doing well."

"So much better than your own mother would do for you, right?" Lacey spouted as she threw her hands in the air.

"And now instead of the problem you're the victim again. Always! I'm so sick of it." Wendy rubbed her forehead.

"Stop yelling at your mother, Wendy," Betty said in the first lull of the argument.

"Why?" Wendy asked, her voice suddenly calm as if she'd somehow found the strength to dial back her frustration.

"Because she deserves your respect," Betty said with a furrowed brow.

Wendy nodded once. "Fine. You're right. I shouldn't have yelled. But I don't take back a thing that I said because it was the truth."

Julia felt she had to interject. She could see where this was going. She'd lived it. Said things that couldn't be taken back. Become estranged from her family for years.

"Wendy, you don't have to stick up for me," Julia said, realizing there was only one way out of this. Her family had already painted Julia as a villain. No matter what she did they would blame everything on her. So if that was going to be the case, she might as well use it. Maybe she could save Wendy's relationship with her family because it seemed Julia didn't have hope for one. At least not the kind of relationship she wished she could have. "Wendy's just saying the things she thinks I would say if I had the nerve."

Lacey nodded as if that was what she'd thought all along. Betty harrumphed as she crossed her arms over her chest.

Right. Nothing new to see here. Just Julia getting frustrated with her blameless mom and sister again.

"Aunt Julia." Wendy turned to her.

Julia gave the tiniest shake of her head. "I get that it took a lot for you two to come and visit us out here. You feel more comfortable at home."

Betty's arms lowered a bit and Lacey's frown became less severe.

"I should have said that earlier. I'm sorry." Julia realized she was truly sorry for that. Yes, the last-minute way in which her mom and sister had come had been bothersome. But that shouldn't negate the fact that they were here when they didn't want to be. Neither liked leaving their small town. They found travel wearying. They were truly just here for Wendy and maybe a little for Julia.

Wendy rubbed a hand against the side of her neck, clearly unsure of what to do now. Julia knew she was debating whether she should take back what Julia had said, let them know it had nothing to do with her aunt, but she had also seen Julia's determination to be the bad guy here.

"I'm sorry too. I shouldn't have yelled and Aunt Julia is right, you two made a huge effort for us. Thank you. I saw all of the complaints instead of seeing the work you put in. But I have to reiterate that nothing I said was Aunt Julia's fault. I was in the wrong but I was in the wrong by myself."

Julia should have known. Price women were too bullheaded to let someone else take the blame.

Betty's arms fell to her sides. "And I guess I could have been more complimentary. But you already know this house is beautiful and grand and that the ocean is marvelous."

Julia did. But to hear her mom say it meant so much. Julia wouldn't hold her breath at getting an apology as well. This was as good as it was going to get when it came to Betty Price.

"The stickiness isn't quite as annoying as I first thought," Lacey added.

And that, ladies and gentlemen, was what Julia was going to call a miracle. This was as close as Lacey would ever get to admitting she'd been wrong.

Wendy looked around the table at the women she loved. Julia, for better or worse, loved them with all of her heart as well.

"Let's dig in," Wendy said.

Julia watched as Betty smiled and Lacey nearly did so

before they all feasted. Betty even had a small serving of curry, giving Julia hope. Because if that tiny change of mindset could happen, then anything could, right?

"YOU COULDN'T HAVE MISSED me as much as I desperately miss you," Julia said later that night when she was tucked into bed, facetiming with Ellis.

His gorgeous mug was a sight for sore eyes even if just on her tiny phone screen.

"Not possible, Sweetheart. I missed you more than any human being could miss another," Ellis said, but his words were interrupted by a jaw-cracking yawn. Julia knew she should let him go. He'd been practicing with his band since early that morning and had another six am wakeup call the next day.

She was getting the tiniest taste of tour and didn't like it. But she loved Ellis and he loved music, so she'd learn to put up with it.

"You don't have to make it a competition," Julia teased.

"No competition. I win, hands down." Ellis grinned.

Ack, she wanted to kiss that grin.

"How was arrival day?" Ellis asked. Even from over two thousand miles away Ellis had tried to help when he'd heard about Julia's family coming to town.

"Terrible, then pretty good, and then kind of hard again," Julia said.

Dinner had gone smoothly after the argument but after Wendy had left it was like the best behavior masks came off and her mom and sister went right back to complaining. The bed was too big, the sheets were too soft. Why was there a couch in the bedroom?

But then again, would they be Betty and Lacey if they didn't complain? Julia wished she could find out.

She giggled to herself.

"What's going on in that pretty head?" Ellis asked.

"Just reliving my night. I'll spare you the details, but we're all in bed with one day down. I'll count that as a victory," Julia said.

"Not everyone likes their family," Ellis said.

Julia knew that. Being estranged from her family had given others license to tell her what was wrong with theirs. She found most families had hardship and drama.

"But I do love them," Julia said, even if at moments she didn't like her family.

"I know that, Love. And you love hard. I'm just counting myself lucky that I get to be a recipient of that love." Ellis said just the right thing.

Chosen family was sometimes so much easier to love.

Then Julia thought of Wendy. Gifted family could also be pretty easy to love as well.

Ellis yawned again and that was Julia's cue. As much as she'd like to keep him on the line until morning, that wasn't fair.

"I love you. Sleep well," Julia said as a farewell.

"I love you, Darling. I always have my phone on me. Call if things get rough."

Julia bit back a laugh. Ellis had heard what Julia had said, right? Things were almost always rough when it came to Betty and Lacey. But it was nice to know that he was there.

"Night," Julia said, drinking in the last moments of getting to see Ellis' face.

"Night."

Julia waited for Ellis to hang up, then slowly set her phone on her bedside table.

Wendy had left that evening to spend time with her new

boyfriend. Lacey and Betty hadn't been happy about it but when Wendy had promised to introduce them to him on this trip, they'd seemed appeased.

But Wendy leaving because she had her own life had had Julia thinking. Wendy would be fine without her. Could Julia go on tour?

Sure, it would be tough to live on the road. But it was just her. She could find stuff to keep herself occupied. And seeing Ellis daily would be worth it, wouldn't it?

She'd never wanted to be one of those women who followed their man around, but now that she was thinking about living that life she could see it wasn't exactly what she'd assumed it would be. Yes, she would be sacrificing this time in her life but Ellis would surely do the same if the situation were reversed. She wasn't a groupie, but a beloved companion. It was only her pride that had her thinking in that old way that a girlfriend who followed her boyfriend wouldn't be respected. Ellis had shown Julia nothing but respect, and he clearly adored her more than anything. So how could she let her pride keep her from being truly content?

Because seeing Ellis, even on tour, would make Julia perfectly and blissfully happy.

With those thoughts, Julia drifted off to sleep.

CHAPTER TEN

"THIS IS NOT what I had in mind when you said you were going to help me feel young and desirable again," Lou said dryly as she and Alexis walked into the go-kart racing facility.

Alexis chuckled. "I'm pretty sure those weren't the words I used."

Alexis had planned an evening out for just the two of them. After Lou's disastrous date, when Jax was no closer to asking her out as she was still taking lessons, Alexis could tell that her best friend was feeling frustrated. She was finally ready to push the go button on her dating life after being hung up on Harvey for so long, but now she couldn't date the man she would have chosen and the man she could date had not only been kind of creepy by wanting Lou to become a replica of his first wife, but he'd insulted her all along the way. Lou's poor self-confidence had taken a hard hit and Alexis was anxious to cheer her up.

And that's why they were about to don completely unflattering helmets and race around the track with high schoolers.

"What I'd said was that I would plan a fun and adventurous night on the town for the two of us," Alexis clarified.

"Yet somehow I heard young and desirable. Maybe

because that's what I was wishing for. Is it too late to switch all of this for a makeover? I was really hoping for a Genovian princess moment. The one when my unibrow would be plucked away and I'd look like the royal I was always meant to be?"

Alexis shook her head as they waited in line at the check-in desk. She didn't answer Lou right away, focused on moving forward in line. As they did so she took in the vast arena, the industrial feel of the place. It was pretty cool, with lots of exposed ducts and piping along the ceiling. The walls all around them were painted a plain white with one bold, black racing stripe. All of the flooring was cement and behind the check-in desk hung black and red racing jackets as well as other gear for sale.

"First, you don't have a unibrow," Alexis said when the line stopped moving and she could concentrate on talking to her best friend.

"That's debatable," Lou said as she touched the skin between her eyebrows. "I haven't plucked or waxed for at least a month."

Alexis rolled her eyes. "And second, you don't need a makeover. You are gorgeous, Lou."

Alexis wished her friend could see in the mirror who Alexis saw in front of her. A stunning, curvy woman. Vibrant and kind and beautiful.

Lou crossed her arms over her chest and harrumphed. But she stopped arguing so Alexis hoped that meant Lou believed what she'd said.

"But I did want to take you out for a night where you could feel like a woman. I know you love being a mom, sister, daughter, friend, business partner, etc. But all of those hats can make it hard to remember that under all of that you are a woman."

"And you thought go-kart racing would help me to feel

womanly?" Lou raised an incredulous eyebrow, uncrossing her arms to prop a hand on one hip.

"It's fun and adventurous," Alexis argued. Maybe this activity was a little out of the box for two women of their age, but the thrill of racing would be just what they needed.

Or at least Alexis hoped.

Because although she had anticipated that they'd be a bit out of place, she hadn't thought they'd be the oldest in the room by at least a dozen years, the majority of the people teenagers.

The group in line just in front of them had to be around fourteen or fifteen, and same with the group farther ahead in line, just about to check in.

Alexis turned to take in the rest of the place. There had to be a group of parents somewhere in here, right?

But as she surveyed the place it was all the same. Groups of boys, girls, and sometimes boys and girls together who all looked too young to drive.

She guessed that made sense. Kids who couldn't drive yet would find this activity the most thrilling. But where were the other adults who were longing for a sense of adventure?

Alexis turned to Lou with her question.

"Getting makeovers and feeling like Genovian princesses," Lou deadpanned.

Alexis laughed.

"We can leave if you want," she offered between her chuckles.

Her discomfort at the ages of kids around her was growing. Her activity looked to be a bust.

"Nah. We're already here, so let's get on the track. If anything, this will earn me major cool mom points with Aiden and Cash," Lou said with a wink.

And this was why Lou was her best friend.

She glanced around the place once more, the go-karts looking tinier than she'd imagined. She knew there were junior karts as well and hoped the ones she was seeing were those. Her ample behind would have some trouble being shoved into that small space.

The next group in line finally all checked in and she and Lou moved up one more space. But with another gaggle of teenagers needing to check in, Alexis knew they'd be waiting for a bit more.

A laugh Alexis recognized all too well suddenly filled her ears.

She shook her head. There was no way.

She and Lou had come by ferry to Seattle since there hadn't been anything like this on the island. And the owner of that laugh, although with her mom for the weekend, should be nowhere near here.

Teenagers all sounded the same, didn't they?

Granted, Brittany was only a preteen or tween. But still. It had to be a coincidence.

Alexis looked to Lou, who was gazing at one of the jackets for sale. See, if Lou hadn't heard it, Alexis must have heard wrong.

There was no way Brittany was here.

Convinced of that, Alexis decided to look at the crowds of teens a little more closely. Just in case.

Alexis glanced from brunette to blond to redhead to raven, the hair and faces all beginning to blend together until one came into view.

No, no, no, no.

But Alexis would recognize even the back of that brown head anywhere. Her eyes scanned over Brittany to see the young girl was wearing way too little. Especially considering the weather. Her white cropped top came nowhere near the top of her tiny denim shorts. Brittany turned to her left and Alexis felt her eyes go wide.

Where had that chest come from? Brittany had to be wearing a pushup bra but Alexis was pretty sure even Marsha wouldn't have bought her seventh grader a pushup bra. Then again, Marsha was a tiny woman all around. Maybe Brittany had stolen one of her mom's bras? Alexis wouldn't put it past Brittany.

Alexis felt her heart pounding even harder than it would have during her race. What was she supposed to do?

For just a moment she let herself think that maybe Marsha had let Brittany come here. Go-kart racing was a wholesome enough activity.

But when Alexis glanced at the rest of Brittany's group, hoping against hope that she'd recognize other girls from Brittany's class, her heart fell.

Boys. Five boys. Not a single one of Brittany's known friends among them and to make matters worse, Brittany would guess these boys were Peter's age, if not older.

So much for the girl being disgusted by the idea of a date. Brittany was a much better actress than Alexis had ever imagined. And Alexis had fallen for the act: hook, line, and sinker.

She groaned internally as she remembered she had been the one to encourage Jared not to pursue learning about Brittany's new boyfriend. She's only twelve, Alexis had said. It had to be an innocent exchange between kids.

Jared was so going to dump her. And Alexis couldn't even blame him. She was tempted to dump her own butt right about now.

Alexis closed her eyes, willing the group to disappear. Wishing and hoping she'd just imagined it all. But when she opened her eyes, they were all still there, busty Brittany in their midst.

"Our turn." Lou nudged Alexis forward. Somehow she'd missed Alexis' entire breakdown.

Alexis just shook her head and pulled Lou out of line. They had much bigger things to attend to now than go-kart racing. Their night of fun had just taken a turn for the not-so-fun.

"What's going on?" Lou asked much too loudly. Brittany would hear.

Alexis hushed Lou, searching for a place where Brittany couldn't see them, but the room was wide open. Unless they hid behind the counter there wasn't a space that wasn't visible to the whole room. Alexis had to settle for dragging her friend to hide behind a group of taller boys.

"You're acting more strangely than normal," Lou whispered, her voice barely audible over the roar of the karts.

"It's Brittany," Alexis whispered back, pointing.

"What?" Lou said loudly, whirling around.

The boys they'd been using as shields gave them both a wary look before moving to the other side of the room. Alexis would have congratulated them for running from the weird strangers were she not so preoccupied with her current situation.

"Shh!" Alexis said urgently. The last thing she wanted was for Brittany to look their way.

"Why are you shushing me? Why are we hiding?" Lou asked a great question.

Alexis, as the adult, knew she shouldn't be the one hiding. And yet, until she understood exactly what was going on she didn't want Brittany to see her.

"And what is she wearing? Why is her little chest so perky?" Lou asked more good questions. But there was no time to share Alexis' Marsha bra theory.

"She needs a coat." Lou began to take hers off as if she was going to march right over there and throw the article of clothing over her niece.

"Just wait a minute," Alexis finally managed.

"Why?" Lou asked, her eyes wide. She wanted to go into full aunt mode.

"Because we don't know what's going on." Alexis needed to gather more information. This was all going to hit the fan but Alexis wanted to be prepared. Maybe then she'd have a chance of righting things when the dust settled? That seemed like hoping for too much but Alexis was feeling desperate.

"I see my twelve-year-old niece with a group of teen boys. Pretty sure I know what's going on," Lou said. Alexis could almost see the steam pouring from her ears.

"Lou, please," Alexis basically begged. "I know you want to go over there and drag Brittany home but the balance in our relationship is so precarious."

"So you're going to ignore this?" Lou asked, her eyes somehow managing to go wider.

"No!" Alexis declared, then quickly lowered her voice. "But if we embarrass Brittany now she may never forgive us."

Lou shrugged a shoulder as if that was a price she was willing to pay.

"Jared is already going to flip out at her. If we take a few breaths maybe we can handle this with some diplomacy," Alexis continued.

She knew her allegiance was to Jared. It always would be. But she also saw more than Lou seemed to. She'd first been shocked by Brittany's appearance as well. But then she remembered another tween girl . . . herself. Alexis at that age would have done just about anything to gain the attention and acceptance of the opposite sex. As a kid who'd been rejected by her dad, Alexis had wanted nothing more than to prove him wrong. To show the world that she was desirable. If given the chance,

Alexis would have done exactly what Brittany had done. And although Brittany had a dad who loved her, the poor girl had been through a lot in the past year or so. Her grandma passing and her grandpa remarrying, her parents' divorce, and then her dad dating a new woman whom her mother hated. Plus her mom had dated a married guy. The list of reasons why Brittany would act out was about a mile long. The last thing Alexis wanted to do was hurt a girl who was obviously already hurting.

She knew Lou would feel the same once she got over the shock of seeing the teen Barbie version of Brittany.

Lou took a deep breath and then another, taking Alexis's advice while looking her in the eye. Alexis could hear Lou's unspoken words. She'd paused to collect herself, and now she wanted to act.

Lou cocked her head as she continued to stare Alexis down. "So what's the plan, then?"

That was another great question. One Alexis had been contemplating ever since she'd first laid eyes on Brittany.

Part of her wanted to call Jared and ask him how she should handle it, but no. She'd been the one to stick her nose into all of this. Jared had said he appreciated her being a part of their parenting process so it was time to put on her big girl pants and get things done. If Jared were here she'd totally let him take the lead, but since he wasn't this was up to Alexis.

Oh, she was going to mess this up so badly.

No, confidence.

She was only going to mess this up a little bit. That felt a lot more like the truth than that she was going to nail this.

"She's holding his hand, Lex," hissed Lou, her eyes now on Brittany and the one of the boys who must be her boyfriend. "If they kiss I'm going postal."

Alexis knew they had to act soon. Would Brittany kiss this boy in a room full of strangers? Alexis didn't want to find out.

She still had no plan but they had to get moving. She offered a quick prayer for help and guidance and began walking toward the group, knowing Lou would follow.

"Hey Brit," Alexis said as she neared Brittany.

Brittany dropped the hand she'd been holding and looked toward Alexis with wide, innocent eyes. Alexis could already see the wheels turning in her head. She was coming up with a game plan that would be full of lies.

"This must be your boyfriend?" Alexis asked, turning to the boy standing next to Brittany. What had Brittany said his name was? Alexis wracked her brain. Drake!

Drake coughed and his friends all looked ready to laugh.

Alexis had thought she was playing it cool. She'd already messed up?

"We don't really do labels," Drake said, looking down from his height at Brittany. But it felt like he was looking down on her in more ways than just the physical.

Brittany took a step back from Drake, toward Alexis. Almost as if this looming boy was suddenly scaring her.

"You and Brittany don't?" Lou asked. She sounded surprisingly calm, considering she'd been about to blow her lid a minute before.

"No. Me and the boys," Drake waved toward his group of friends.

He'd already acknowledged them ten times more than he had Brittany and Alexis had watched as Brittany seemed to shrink with every word and movement Drake made. She understood how flippant he was being about her, how little he seemed to care.

Brittany had moved away from her boyfriend until she now stood beside Alexis, her eyes full of pain. Alexis would bet that this boy acted much differently in private and Brittany was just now getting to see this side of him.

"Hm," Alexis said. An ache for the lying but hurt girl next to her welled up, spurring her on. "So what would you call what's going on between you and Brittany?"

Drake shrugged, his focus on his friends, almost as if he'd forgotten who had asked him the question. "We've been having fun." He made a crude gesture and his friends all began laughing. The sound that should have been delightful sounded cruel to Alexis' ears.

Alexis just had to hope that Brittany didn't understand the motion.

Alexis took a step forward, her shoulder sharply bumping into Drake's. The sudden movement caught them all off guard and the other boys stopped laughing abruptly.

"How old are you?" Alexis asked, pinning Drake with a glare that had him fidgeting. Good.

"Fifteen," he said without any hesitation, telling Alexis Brittany had to have lied about her own age. Granted, with that pushup bra Brittany looked pretty dang close to fifteen. Too close.

"I'm going to tell you something that all little boys should know," Alexis said, her voice firm and commanding. From their squirming she knew all of the boys were feeling uneasy. "Women and girls should never be used. Ever." Alexis pointed a finger at Drake's chest and fought the urge to poke him. "Girls deserve respect. You are not cool because you use girls for your 'fun.' You are not 'the man' because you string them along, leading them to think one thing while you are telling your friends something entirely different. You are all little boys. And until you learn to respect women, you will always be just that. Do you understand?" Alexis asked. Her eyes were focused on the one boy who'd used Brittany but the message was for all.

"Yeah," Drake muttered, his eyes downcast. Alexis heard more mumbled responses behind him.

"Now get out of here," Alexis said as she shooed them away with her hand. Even though she'd come in planning to play it cool, when she saw what was really going on, there was no way she would allow that boy near Brittany ever again. As much as she hadn't wanted to embarrass the girl, standing up for her and teaching those misguided teens a lesson had become more important.

The boys obeyed instantly, scattering as soon as they had a chance and leaving Lou, Alexis, and Brittany alone.

Alexis drew in a deep breath, exhaust filling her lungs from the go-karts. But she needed the fortification before she turned to see what Brittany was going to say. Alexis had become that overbearing, overprotective lioness of a mother even after she'd promised herself she was going to play it cool. Yet she couldn't bring herself to feel sorry about it. Brittany had needed a protector even if she hadn't wanted one. The girl had tons of friends. What she'd needed right then was not a friend but a grown woman who would do whatever she could to keep Brittany safe.

Brittany looked from Lou to Alexis, tears glittering in her eyes. Alexis pushed her shoulders back, bracing herself. A tantrum of the tween sorts was brewing. Alexis had butted in, lectured those teen boys that Brittany had cared so much about, and then shooed them away. Brittany may have been hurt by how Drake had treated her but she would be completely mortified by the way Alexis had handled things. Alexis was ready to hear phrases like *You aren't my mother. I hate you. I hope my dad breaks up with you!*

But without a word Brittany took a step toward Alexis as the tears began to run down her cheeks, causing her mascara to stream down her face. Now that Alexis was close she could see Brittany had caked the stuff on. Probably in another attempt to look older.

"I'm so sorry," Brittany suddenly said, her breath catching.

Alexis glanced at Lou, whose mouth hung open. This wasn't what either of them were expecting.

Brittany suddenly began sobbing and when Alexis held out her arms, Brittany fell into them, letting Alexis hold her while she wept.

"He said he was falling in love with me. But he was just using me for fun?" Brittany's voice squeaked. "I lied about being fourteen but his lie was worse, wasn't it?"

Alexis just held Brittany and let her speak. She was pretty sure Brittany wasn't waiting for an answer.

"I didn't even kiss him." Brittany pulled back to look Alexis in the face before burying her head in the crook of Alexis's arm once more. "He made it seem like we went all the way or something. Just so he could look cool to his friends."

The fact that she couldn't even say 'sex' reminded Alexis of how young this little girl still was. She acted strong and tough, much too mature for her years, but she was still a child, barely out of elementary school, being preyed on by much older boys.

"He was using me, wasn't he?" she whispered.

Another rhetorical question, but Alexis nodded.

Alexis was furious with Drake but had to remind herself that the boy was still just fifteen too. They were kids trying to play with parts of life that should be reserved for grownups, for people mature enough to handle the emotions behind the physical acts.

"Please take me home," Brittany requested between sobs.

So Alexis did just that.

ALEXIS HAD LEFT Brittany in the car with Lou while she went in to talk with Jared. When she'd offered to take Brittany to her mom's, Brittany had just shaken her head.

"I want to see Dad," she'd said.

So Alexis had brought her to Jared's home. But she wasn't about to bring everyone in until she'd warned Jared of what was coming. She knew the several stages of emotions she'd personally traveled since seeing Brittany at the go-kart arena. She wanted Jared to get through a few before Brittany came in so that she wouldn't have to witness them all.

Yes, the girl deserved to be punished. Grounded for a month or more for lying about so many things and meeting up with boys she knew were much older. But she'd already been so hurt. Alexis didn't want Jared, however inadvertent it may be, to pile on top of that hurt.

"What are you doing here?" Jared asked as he spun Alexis into his home, kicking the door closed behind her.

He kissed her so deeply her toes curled and she let herself revel in the kiss for a few moments. After Jared heard what had happened that evening who knew when he'd be kissing her again? Or even if he'd be kissing her again.

Alexis didn't want to believe that Jared would break up with her because of what had happened but people had broken up for far less. And Jared was so protective of Brittany. Alexis would almost understand if he did so. He wanted to keep his family safe, and because of Alexis' interference he hadn't.

But Alexis couldn't focus on that now. Right now was about Brittany and her hurt. The poor girl had cried through the entire ferry ride; her tears had only dried when she'd come into view of her house.

Brittany had taken a deep, shaky breath and unbuckled her seatbelt, but Alexis had asked her to stay so that she could talk to Jared first.

"Thank you," Brittany had said, genuine caring shining through her eyes.

Alexis smiled. At least some good had come out of this terrible evening. It seemed that Brittany had truly come to accept her as a parental figure. Just in time for Jared to break up with her.

Alexis pulled away from Jared's kiss, already missing his lips.

"The kids are at Marsha's tonight," Jared said with a wriggle of his eyebrows.

Oh, how Alexis wished she was free to capitalize on that offer. But she had to move to the business at hand.

"I'm actually here on—" Alexis wasn't sure what to call it.

"Is everything okay?" Jared asked, one eyebrow raised. His characteristic look of concern.

Alexis shook her head. "I brought Brittany with me," she said before she explained the events that had transpired that evening.

His anger grew as the story went on, and Alexis could see the moment that his fury switched from Brittany to the boy.

"What was his name?" Jared asked through barely concealed anger.

"Drake." Alexis answered all she could, grateful she'd never learned a last name. She knew Jared wanted to track him down. Luckily for the boy, Alexis was pretty sure he wasn't from the island.

Jared scrubbed a hand over his face.

"I'm so sorry." Alexis felt she needed to say this before Brittany joined them. As soon as she was there the conversation would become all about her, as it rightfully should. But Alexis needed Jared to know she hadn't meant for things to get so out of control.

"Why are you sorry? You were there for my baby girl.

Sticking up for her. I should be saying thank you." Jared pulled Alexis into his arms. "Thank you, Alexis."

He'd be singing a different tune soon. Maybe he'd forgotten what Alexis had said before about the boy?

"I was the one who said it wasn't a big deal with her phone. That it had to be an innocent interaction between kids. I was wrong—this boy was a big deal. He could have really messed with Brit." Alexis shuddered to think what would have happened had she not ended up at that go-kart racing place tonight.

"What you saw was exactly what it looked like from the information we had. Parenting 101, Lex, you can only work with what you're given. And we were given very little. Orchestrated nicely by Brittany, no doubt. I'm so grateful you were there for Brit tonight too, but not to right your wrong. You did the best you could before. We both did the best we could. We're bound to make mistakes."

"So you aren't going to dump me?" Alexis asked. She held her breath, heart racing.

Jared shook his head so hard Alexis worried he'd dislodge something. But his answer was adamantly clear and Alexis wanted to cheer.

"Not a chance," Jared said as he drank in the sight of his girlfriend. "You continue to astonish me at every turn, Alexis. There is no woman on earth who could compare to the woman you are. The woman you are to me."

Alexis wanted to kiss him right then, but they had other matters to tend to. Brittany. And Lou. The poor woman hadn't gotten anything Alexis had promised her that evening.

Jared went to open the door before turning back and pulling Alexis back into his arms, pressing a kiss to her forehead. "Better ones are coming, but if I claim those lips now, Brit will be waiting out there for hours."

Alexis grinned. She liked the sound of that. Well, not the Brit waiting but the hours part. Kissing Jared into the night sounded heavenly.

Jared suddenly let her go and opened the door, waving toward the car.

The sound of two doors slamming sounded and Alexis waited behind Jared.

Brittany entered the house first, thankfully wearing Lou's coat. Alexis hadn't even thought to warn Jared about his daughter's outfit but thankfully that conversation could wait for later since Brittany was now covered adequately. Alexis wasn't sure Jared could handle the sight of Brittany's outfit after hearing about what had already happened that evening.

"Daddy," Brittany said as she collapsed into her father's hug.

Thankfully Jared seemed to be expecting that reaction and was ready to cradle his daughter. Seeing Brittany all bundled up in the coat, looking so small next to Jared's frame, Alexis found it hard to believe this was the same girl who'd confidently held a high school boy's hand just hours before.

"I'm sorry about how your evening went," Alexis whispered to Lou, who stood just outside the door.

Lou shook her head. "I'm just so glad we were there."

Of course Lou would feel that way. She loved Brittany fiercely too. They all worried for their wild one.

"And you can make it up to me. Except next time I want the Genovian princess makeover," Lou said with a grin and a wink.

Alexis muffled her laugh before turning back to see that Jared and Brittany had left the foyer.

"Whatever you say, Your Highness." Alexis gave the worst curtsy ever.

She then remembered that Lou was stuck at Jared's because Alexis had been the one to drive them to Seattle. But now that their night was blown, Alexis was sure Lou would rather go home to her kids.

"Take my car," she offered, handing her keys to Lou. "I think I'll stay here for a bit."

"And then let Jared take you home after the best makeout session of your life?" Lou asked with a smirk.

"Get out of here." Alexis gave her friend a playful shove even though she'd only voiced exactly what Alexis was hoping.

"Oh, and the coat was a nice touch," Alexis said to a retreating Lou.

"Thought we should spare Jared the heart attack," Lou said.

Alexis nodded. That was exactly what Lou had done.

After Lou drove off, Alexis shut the door and turned to look for Brittany and Jared.

She didn't have to go far. She heard their voices as soon as she left the foyer.

"I'm taking it back," Jared said firmly. He stood with his arms crossed over his chest, but watched his daughter calmly, keeping his emotions under control.

Brittany nodded from her seat on the couch, seeming repentant.

"Just a flip phone until you're fourteen. And I'm reading all of your texts," Jared added.

Brittany nodded again. Her eyes shone with already shed tears but other than that she didn't even look disappointed. It was as if she'd expected or maybe even hoped for as much. The phone had been too much freedom, too much responsibility for her twelve-year-old brain and she was relieved to have more manageable boundaries.

"How did you meet that boy?" Jared asked.

Brittany didn't even hesitate before blurting out the whole story. "At the movies in Seattle, like two months ago. I went with Mom but she was on a date. I wanted to watch this action movie but she wanted to see the new chick flick with her guy. So she told me I could go by myself. Drake noticed the open seat next to me and took it. We started talking and when he told me he was fifteen, I said I was fourteen. He asked me for my number."

Alexis was going to guess that was the dad-friendly version of what had happened but she wasn't going to push Brittany to say more. The fact that she was being so honest now was huge for the girl.

"And today is the only other time you've seen him?" Jared asked.

Brittany nodded. "We just texted until today."

Jared narrowed his eyes as he observed his daughter for a long moment but then nodded once. "And what have you learned from what happened tonight?" Jared asked.

Brittany wiped under her eyes, the sad things rimmed with black thanks to her running mascara.

"That boys are terrible and they're liars," Brittany said as she sniffed.

Jared nodded.

Alexis nudged Jared. He couldn't let that stand. While Brittany needed to learn to be careful, she also needed to know that good men were out there so she didn't settle for another jerk.

"Not all boys are liars and terrible. Just most of them. So trust your dad on some of this stuff," Jared said before cracking his neck.

Not quite what Alexis had had in mind, but it would do. Right now they were all pretty disillusioned with teen boys.

"Anything else?" Jared asked.

"That Alexis has my back," Brittany said, turning to Alexis.

Alexis startled.

What had Brittany said?

"I know you're mad at me and it seems like I'm saying this

just so you'll be a little less mad but I promise that's not why. I'm glad Alexis was there and told Drake and his friends off. It's what I wanted to do but was too scared. Alexis is pretty cool, Dad," Brittany said.

Oh no, don't cry now. The last thing Alexis wanted to do was make Brittany regret her words.

"I know," Jared answered, his voice sounding a little less parental.

"I overheard Mom telling her friend that you're waiting on me and Peter before you take the next step with Alexis."

Brittany needed to stop snooping. She was hearing messages much too mature for her young ears.

"Is the next step marriage?" Brittany asked, looking from her dad to Alexis.

Alexis was going to let Jared field that one.

"It is," he said without a moment's hesitation.

Alexis bit her lip to keep from beaming. She'd thought so too, but to hear Jared tell his daughter so confidently made her heart rejoice.

"Okay," Brittany said, standing. "Can I go to my room?"

Wait, what did that 'okay' mean? They needed clarification. Was Alexis getting married?!

"What does 'okay' mean?" Apparently Jared was just as eager to know as Alexis.

Thank goodness.

"I know you don't need my permission. But if you're waiting for me to be okay with it, I'm okay. You can marry Alexis," Brittany said matter-of-factly as if she weren't handing Alexis the moon and the stars.

She knew Jared would have eventually proposed even if Brittany was against the marriage. But it would have been a battle instead of a lovely union. And Alexis wasn't sure if she could have accepted. Saying yes would have put such a strain on

Jared's relationship with his children. Could she have done that to Jared? And to herself, knowing the difficulties that would bring to her new marriage?

But now they wouldn't have to make that decision. Even though they'd still surely have issues, having Brittany's blessing was better than she could have ever hoped for.

Alexis would have never guessed that's how this would have ended.

"Thank you, Brittany," Alexis had to say even if Brittany would call her cringey.

But she didn't. She just smiled at Alexis before turning to her dad, waiting for his answer.

"Yeah, you can go to your room," Jared said as Brittany handed him her phone without even being asked.

Brittany ran out of the living room, leaving Jared and Alexis staring at one another.

Alexis suddenly realized that maybe this was too much for Jared. Maybe he had more reservations about their next step than just his kids' opinion. And Peter still hadn't given his okay. Granted, they both knew he would be the easier of the two kids. If Brittany was fine, Peter wouldn't care.

"You don't have to propose, you know," Alexis said, giving Jared an out.

"I know," Jared said, a twinkle in his eyes.

What did that mean?

"I'm not expecting anything," Alexis reiterated.

Except that was a lie. She had kind of been expecting something. Before Jared's reaction, anyway.

Jared moved until his chest was practically touching Alexis'. If she took a deep breath they would.

"The only reason I don't want you to expect anything is because I want my proposal to be a surprise. I want to thrill and shock you, but one thing I need you to know?" Jared said before putting his arms around Alexis' waist. "Never, ever doubt my love for you. What I feel for you is everlasting. It had to be put on hold a few times because of life's situations but not because it ever waned or lacked. I love you, Alexis. Forever and ever."

Alexis nodded but her answer was cut short by Jared's lips finally claiming hers in the way she'd been dreaming of ever since their last kiss. Alexis had a feeling he was making good on his earlier promise and she couldn't have been more delighted.

CHAPTER ELEVEN

"YOU'VE GOT IT, PRESTON!" Lou yelled across the field.

It was their first game since her date with C.J. and things had gone relatively well. Meaning, C.J. had ignored her even when she had smiled in his direction.

Lou took it as a lesson that not much had changed from the last time she'd dated. Things still got awkward after a bad date.

But she knew one thing. She would never let it affect her coaching. She would still treat Preston the way she always had.

Lou felt her parents behind her. They'd become staples at the soccer field for each of Cash's games. Alexis and Jared weren't able to make it to this game because Peter had a parent meeting at the school, but they would typically be there as well.

She knew Bill and Margie were wondering if Jax would show up. Lou was wondering the same. It was a possibility, because at the last game he had asked about the date and time of this game, but Lou had no idea what to think anymore. He'd seemed so interested in her and her family a week ago but then he'd just disappeared. Granted, he'd had no reason to appear in her life. They only had lessons every other week and for some reason her work schedule and Jax's gym routine hadn't seemed to cross paths this week. With all of that time apart Lou couldn't help but wonder if he regretted what he'd said. A very real part of her even wondered if she'd dreamed the entire conversation up. It did seem too good to be true.

Lou was suddenly pulled from her thoughts when in her peripheral vision she noticed people walking from the parking lot toward the field. She fought the urge to look in that direction, forcing her eyes to remain on her team even though she was too distracted to notice what they were doing at the moment. Could it be Jax? Walking with another set of parents? Because although Lou couldn't tell very well who was there, she was pretty sure she'd counted three people.

Trying to focus on the game and her coaching responsibilities, Lou watched as Preston lost the ball and the other team began taking it toward their goal. When they were close, Cash stole the ball back and then both teams seemed to just hang around in the middle of the field, neither side making progress. Seven-year-old soccer could move so slowly and typically Lou loved that about it. But today she wished the action was a bit more interesting because without her full attention on the field . . . against her will, she glanced to the group walking toward her.

The moment she saw them, she wished she hadn't. Her heart nearly stopped at the sight.

What were *they* doing here? She almost asked herself how they knew about the game but then remembered she'd sent Harvey a schedule at the beginning of the season, hoping he'd surprise them all and actually show up for his child.

Lou's mouth went dry as she tried to force her attention back to the action on the field, her weight shifting from one foot to the other.

Cash was taking the ball toward the goal and Lou wanted to cheer for him. It was what she did. But her throbbing throat and dry mouth wouldn't allow it.

Lou knew she should have accepted that *she* could show up too. Harvey wouldn't have come without his new girlfriend. But why here? Why now? Lou hadn't been ready to see Harvey and Felicity together. It almost felt like they were making a statement.

She glanced back to see Harvey and Felicity sit on the far side of her parents, calling her kids over to them. They each approached timidly, Emma last, glancing back at her mom before she did so.

Lou gave her oldest a slight nod of encouragement and Emma finally greeted her dad and Felicity. Lou noticed Bill's hawk eyes on the situation. He'd make sure her kids were okay, so she decided she'd better focus once more on the game.

Cash shot on goal and just missed. Lou clapped her hands, willing her voice to work as she opened her mouth. "Nice try!" she barely managed. She couldn't even add Cash's name.

Cash looked to her, disappointment covering his face. Lou knew it was mostly directed at missing the goal, but Lou couldn't help but direct some of that disappointment toward herself. She was failing Cash. She needed to forget about Harvey and Felicity—she'd know soon enough why they were here—and coach her team, especially her son.

But how was she supposed to do that?

"You'll get it next time, Cash," a familiar voice cheered, buoying Lou's spirits.

He was back.

Lou turned around to see Jax set up behind her, just as he'd been last game. Almost as if he were her second line of defense. She was sure that wasn't why he'd sat there, but it made her feel better, regardless. And Lou felt herself smiling. Her smile only widened after the wink Jax sent her way.

She'd been so distracted by the sight of Harvey and Felicity that she'd completely missed the third person who'd been walking behind them. She wasn't sure how she could have missed the one person in the world she most wanted to see, but he was here now. And Lou felt a little less like she was going to fall over onto her face.

She could do this.

And she did. She cheered and coached and high-fived with the best of them, her spirits rising with each smile her kids gave her.

"Thanks, Coach Lou!" Preston called out at the end of the game before heading for his dad.

Lou gave C.J. a small, polite wave that he ignored.

Oh well.

Lou saw her team off and took a fortifying breath. She knew what she had to do now. Cash had immediately run over to his dad and Felicity, ecstatic that his dad had come to watch him play. It really took so little for their kids to feel appreciated and loved.

What she wanted to do was go to Jax. To give him her heartfelt thanks for coming. She doubted he knew how much she'd needed him . . . she hadn't even known how much she needed him until he was there.

But Jax, if he stuck around, would have to be greeted later.

Lou closed her eyes as she passed her parents. She could feel their concern and care as she made her way to where Harvey and Felicity had set up their beach chairs.

Lou scanned through her possible responses before she arrived. She could say something nice. No one would blame her for being snarky. She could be timid.

As she leaned down to give Cash a congratulatory hug, she decided on cordial.

"Good to see you here," Lou said, partially honest. She wanted Harvey to be there for his kids. But she wished they hadn't made quite the spectacle by coming to Harvey's first game of the season together.

Lou stayed on her knees, gathering her kids around her on either side. She noticed that even though they were happy to see their dad, they felt more comfortable staying close to her.

"Thanks for letting us know about the game," Harvey said.

This was the best conversation they'd had in years. Okay, that might be a slight exaggeration but not much.

But they were trying. Both of them. That was pretty remarkable, considering their past.

Harvey shot the kids a look and then glanced at Lou. Even though they hadn't been happily married for years, Lou understood his unspoken request.

"Hey kiddos. How about you go over and see Grandpa and Grandma Margie," Lou suggested before dropping her arms.

Hazel shot away, not needing to be asked twice.

"Oh yeah. I forgot to tell them about Brittany's new phone. It's so cool. It flips open *and* flips closed," Aiden said before rushing off.

They'd all spent time at Marsha's today so Brittany must have showed them all the consequences of her actions. She'd heard Jared had been stern but Brittany had taken her punishment with grace. Lou was glad Brittany had seen a bright side to getting a relic of a phone. Emma followed Aiden but Cash glanced from his mom to his dad, hesitating. He'd been the one missing his dad most and probably worried he'd disappear again if he did as Lou had asked.

"I promise we'll have lots more time together, Buddy," Harvey said as he patted Cash on the shoulder.

"Soon?" Cash asked. He'd gotten a boatload of empty promises from Harvey before. He was trying to pin him down.

Harvey nodded and only then did Cash walk away, but he still seemed reluctant.

As Cash left, Lou wondered if she should acknowledge Felicity. Maybe? She was considering her next words when Harvey spoke. Thank goodness.

"Felicity and I have been talking about it and we want to see the kids more often," Harvey said.

His words were all very neutral. He wasn't accepting blame for the reasons why he hadn't seen the kids—he'd never shown up—but he wasn't blaming Lou either, so for now she'd let it go.

"That sounds good," Lou said instead of adding that she'd been asking for this for over a year now. She would play nice. For the sake of her kids.

"I know I didn't fight you on any of the custody stuff," Harvey added.

Because he'd been too busy trying to make sure he got more than his fair share of the money. But again Lou kept her thoughts to herself.

"But I thought you'd want me to see the kids," Harvey said.

Lou nodded. "I do."

And she really did. Cash was the only one who outwardly talked about missing his dad, but she knew the others thought about him and could use his influence in their lives. Harvey could be a great dad, when he put in the time. And even though she didn't trust Felicity at all, she trusted Harvey's ability as a father.

Even so, she'd be asking some pretty pointed questions after each visit with Harvey. If she heard anything from her kids she didn't like, she'd be using her custody arrangement to keep her kids far from their father and his girlfriend.

"We thought we could take them to the movies next weekend. And maybe bowling the weekend after that," Harvey stated as if it was already a done deal.

It wasn't, but Lou would consider it.

"You don't have to be a Disneyland dad, you know. You could just have them come over to your house," Lou stated.

"Our tiny apartment? No way. Not until Harvey finds us a real house with a yard," Felicity interjected with a flip of her brown hair. Lou would have been annoyed if the words didn't seem like a dig toward Harvey.

As petty as it was, Lou was a little vindicated to see that it wasn't all cupcakes in Harvey and Felicity world.

"The movies and bowling sound great. But if you don't mind I won't be telling the kids anything until just before each event." Lou refrained from adding her reasoning: she wouldn't be telling the kids because Harvey had canceled so many time she didn't want to raise her kids' hopes for nothing.

Harvey nodded once, surely understanding Lou's underlying message.

Felicity suddenly stood, closing her chair. She'd probably reached her max capacity of acting cordial toward Lou. Lou didn't blame her. She was pretty much there as well.

"I'll text you the movie time by Friday," Harvey promised.

Lou would believe it when she saw it. But they were here. Lou would give them credit for that even if it had made her feel uncomfortable at first.

They didn't say their goodbyes as they gathered their things and Lou walked away. They weren't friends, nor did they want to be, so why pretend a relationship that wasn't there?

"So?" Bill asked when Lou walked toward her parents. Her kids were out of earshot because they were using Jax as a jungle gym.

"What are you guys doing?" Lou yelled to them.

"Jax said it was okay!" Emma yelled back.

Well, if Jax approved it. Lou figured if her conversation with the man hadn't been imagined and he really wanted to one day date her, her kids were a part of the deal, and this was a real representation of who they were. And if the conversation had been imagined, who cared?

"Harvey wants to spend time with them," Lou said quietly for the adult ears.

"Of course he does. First he bleeds you of every last dime and now he wants time with the kids free of charge," her dad muttered.

Bill wasn't Harvey's biggest fan.

"Let's not get too upset. Lou is okay," Margie pointed out to her husband when he started getting red around the ears.

And Lou was. She'd always ended up being okay, thanks to her family. Her dad had always kept her employed, even when he maybe shouldn't have. They'd also helped her to keep her house. Her dad had been there every step of the way and seen the way Harvey had tried to wound Lou at each turn, so he had every right to be bitter. So did Lou.

But that bitterness would hurt her kids. So Lou had to let it go.

"The kids want to see him." Lou gave her reason for not being upset.

Margie nodded and Bill grunted.

"But if he steps out of line I won't hesitate to revoke every right he has when it comes to my kids," Lou said confidently for her dad's sake.

And she felt pretty confident . . . surprisingly. She guessed she really had grown from the woman Harvey had left. Thank heavens.

"And I'll finally get to use that new shotgun I've been saving for a special occasion," Bill joked. At least, Lou was pretty sure he was joking.

Lou decided to leave it alone and turned to Jax, who was laughing under a pile of her children.

She loved how easygoing he was.

"Get off him," Lou directed and reluctantly each kid moved, Cash last. He was not only craving time with his dad but any interaction like this one.

Lou tried not to look too adoringly at Jax. She couldn't quite explain her gratitude that he'd given Cash and the other kids what they'd needed. He hadn't been asked—heck it hadn't even been anticipated—he'd just done it. Because it was who he was. As if Lou needed any more reasons to admire Jax.

She glanced away when she realized she had failed. She was sure her gaze was full of so much adoration no one could mistake what she already felt for the man, including her little Hazel. And the last thing she needed was for her kids to start asking how many dates Lou needed to go on with Jax before the two of them got married. Although the idea of marrying Jax created quite a different reaction in Lou than the idea of marrying Preston's dad.

"Can we get ice cream?" Cash asked when his human jungle gym was no longer an option. His siblings on his heels, he ran to his grandparents, knowing exactly who to ask.

"Why not?" Bill looked at each of his smiling grandkids.

Lou rolled her eyes. Her dad might be a hard man when it came to Harvey, but he was complete mush for his grandkids.

The kids ran toward the parking lot, yelling and cheering as Bill and Margie tried to keep up with them.

Jax and Lou looked on as the rambunctious bunch left them behind.

"Walk you to your car?" Jax offered, his presence beside her strong and sure. He didn't ask anything of her. They hadn't even really greeted one another, and yet it all felt normal. No, it was better than normal—it felt right.

"Sure," Lou said with a grin.

They walked side by side, following the steps of Lou's family, their shoulders nearly brushing. Their fingertips did every few steps and Jax once allowed his pinky to linger a little longer, wrapping it around Lou's for the shortest of seconds and causing her to sweat and freak out in a way no grown woman should at a simple finger touch. Thankfully the interaction was brief or Lou's heart just might have melted within her chest from overuse.

"Your chat with your ex looked pretty intense," Jax said suddenly.

The statement should have surprised Lou. It had seemingly come out of nowhere. And yet, it hadn't. What *had* surprised Lou was that instead of sounding offended that she hadn't greeted him before going straight to Harvey, Jax had sounded . . . concerned. Almost protective.

Lou fought back the emotions those thoughts elicited and tried to keep her mind clear so that she could have an actual conversation with this man. He deserved that much.

Lou shrugged. "He hasn't been involved for a long time. Now he wants to be." It was easiest to stick to the facts.

"How do you feel about that?"

So much for sticking to the facts. With anyone else Lou might have bushed the question aside or answered it briefly. But she found herself wanting to open up to Jax so she didn't hold back.

"It was okay . . . surprisingly. We have a terrible relationship. We haven't been able to talk to one another in months. So the fact that he's here, trying—that's huge. I'm trying to give him credit for that even though it's what every dad should be doing." Lou shook her head, trying to rid herself of the frustration she felt every time she thought about the ways she and Harvey had failed their children.

Jax gazed at Lou with soft eyes, his lips parted and his face full of wonder before he spoke. "For what it's worth, I'm proud of your reaction. I've heard a little of what you've endured from your ex through the grapevine and I'm impressed that you're even willing to acknowledge him. You're amazing."

A compliment from Jax felt like sitting in a peaceful field of beautiful honeysuckle. It not only sounded great, but it looked divine and felt incredible. Lou tried to brush it off, feeling unworthy. "I wouldn't be if it weren't for my kids."

"Then they're lucky," Jax said doing the pinky wrapping thing one more time and causing Lou's heart to race again.

"So you've been keeping up with me through the grapevine?" Lou had meant to tease Jax but it sounded desperate more than anything else.

Jax chuckled. "What can I say? You're a fascinating woman. And I want to know everything about you."

He lowered his voice for the last sentence and Lou felt the sudden urge to lurch forward and close the distance between them, pressing her lips against his.

"Is that why you're here?" Lou asked instead of following through on her fantasy.

"When I shouldn't be? Yeah," Jax said, dropping his head as if he'd been too weak to stay away.

Lou wanted to assure him if this was him being weak, she loved it.

"I tried to get out of lessons," Lou said, wanting Jax to know he wasn't the only one having difficulty staying away. She wanted to date him as much as he wanted to date her. In fact, she imagined she wanted to date him very much more.

"I tried to tell myself my 'no dating students' rule didn't matter," Jax replied.

"Really?" Lou asked. She knew that Jax's rules meant a lot to him. Even if he couldn't change things, the fact that he'd considered it was huge.

Jax nodded.

They arrived at Lou's car far too quickly, but thankfully all of her kids had continued into the parking lot to ride with Grandpa and Grandma Margie so she and Jax were still alone.

"But the bright side is that I still get to see you tomorrow," Jax said, reminding Lou about their lessons the next day.

That was a pretty nice bright side.

"And if you can come for an hour instead of half an hour, I'd love to give you lessons separate from Emma's," Jax said.

Lou shook her head even though the extra time with Jax sounded amazing. But there was no way she could afford another lesson, even at Jax's discounted rate. Nor would she take advantage of whatever this was growing between them and accept free lessons.

"Please? Don't worry about the cost or that you're using me because of the way I feel for you. You wouldn't be. Believe me, I am doing this for completely selfish reasons," Jax said, easing Lou's exact concerns. "Because the further you get along in your playing and the faster you do it, the sooner you can be done being my student."

When he put it that way, with that cute grin tugging at his lips and those green eyes of his capturing Lou's, there was almost no way to say no. She found herself nodding.

"Good," Jax said before stepping back.

"Until tomorrow," he added, his accent somehow making the statement even sexier.

"Until tomorrow," Lou responded, sounding nowhere near as good as Jax had, but judging by his wide smile he didn't care.

Jax walked away as Lou got into her car. She bit her lip and it almost felt like her skin was glowing, she felt so completely alive. If this was what Jax could do to her with a single conversation maybe it was a good thing they couldn't date until she was a little more immune to his charms.

Who was she kidding? Jax had the kind of charm that no immunity could guard against. She was pretty sure she would forever be captured by it, by him. She couldn't wait to see if she was right about her theory.

But as much as Lou craved to have more with Jax she found herself somehow still satisfied. Just knowing he really, truly wanted to date her was enough . . . for now.

CHAPTER TWELVE

"YOU'LL BE the prettiest woman in the room," Mack said, coming up behind Nora as she did her last primping before going out the door.

About a week before, Genevieve had decided that she wanted a couples' wedding shower. Not only had she told Elise and Amber that she expected it to be held at the inn within a week's time, but she wanted the girls to host it as well. To say the inn had been in a flurry of preparations would have been the understatement of the year.

And as the cherry on top on that terrifying sundae, Genevieve had asked Nora to finalize a few of her paintings so that she could see them before the big day. So not only had the girls been in over their heads with all they had to do, but Nora had her own concerns that kept her stomach in a ball of nerves.

But now the night was here. And ready or not, they were all going to have to put on a show.

"You do realize that there will be literal movie stars in the room," Nora said with a grin as she turned toward Mack. How he could calm her nerves even on a night like this she'd never understand, but she was incredibly grateful for it. "Now you, my boyfriend," Nora hummed as she scanned Mack from his hypnotic blue eyes to his shiny dress shoes, taking in his form-fitting button-up and navy blue slacks. The man was a delight to look at. "You'll put them all to shame."

Mack chuckled, the sound low and all too pleasant. So pleasant that if it weren't for the biggest commission Nora had ever dreamed of hanging in the balance, Nora would have blown the evening off.

But Genevieve would never forgive Nora if she were a no-show. Neither would Nora's girls, considering the seating at the event was all arranged and having an empty chair would be close to the worst thing imaginable. At least that was what Elise had said earlier that day.

Elise and Amber were afraid that, due to the distance almost all of Genevieve's guests would have to travel, at the last minute many of them wouldn't show. Not to mention invites had gone out barely a week before. Genevieve had assured the girls that none of that would be a problem. A party in her honor would be the kind of coveted invitation that people would move moun-tains to get to Whisling for, but the girls were doubtful. Emer-gencies happened as well as prior engagements people couldn't escape, although the RSVP rate had been nearly one hundred percent, something the girls hadn't expected. But instead of breathing easier it had caused Amber to nearly hyperventilate. Now they had to plan on everyone but the reality that they'd all show seemed slim at best.

"No one will even notice me when I'm next to you," Mack said as he gathered Nora in his arms and then kissed her neck, the only exposed portion of her body that wasn't covered by makeup.

The kiss sent shivers down her spine and she reluctantly pulled away. If she stayed where she was there was an eighty percent chance she'd arrive to the wedding shower with makeup and hair askew. And a fifty percent chance she wouldn't show at all.

Instead, Nora hung a simple silver hoop from her earlobe. The dress code for the evening was island style. The actual wedding was a black tie event but Genevieve had wanted a more comfortable experience for the shower. So Nora had dug through her closet to find a long and flowy light brown dress dotted with tiny mustard yellow and white flowers. Island yet fall. She hoped she was dressed up enough. She'd asked Amber and Elise what they were wearing but because they were working the event they felt it best they both show up in their little black dresses.

"What if she hates the paintings?" Nora suddenly voiced her biggest concern of the evening. Yes, she was worried she was underdressed or, more importantly, that people wouldn't show and the girls would have to figure out what to do then, but the biggest fear on her mind was her paintings. Genevieve had paid her a king's ransom for these watercolors; what if she didn't live up to Genevieve's expectations?

Mack stepped up so he was just behind Nora again, gently encircling her waist with his arms. "Impossible," he said into Nora's hair.

More shivers. The man had a talent.

"She's the one who sought you out. She knows what you do —she saw the sample painting at Julia's," Mack assured as he held on tight.

"One painting," Nora countered.

"And the simple mockups you sent her for the wedding. She'd have to be blind, dumb, or both to be anything but impressed."

Nora bit her lip, knowing she'd have to redo her lipstick, but she couldn't help it. "Really?" she finally asked before touching up her lips.

"Really," Mack said confidently and Nora had to believe him.

Because Mack was not only smart, he was gifted when it came to art. In the gallery they both worked in, Mack always knew which paintings would sell to which customers. It was why he was top salesman again and again, even as Nora worked her butt off to beat him.

"Thank you," Nora said as she tucked her lipstick into her purse and put on her white sandals. Her feet would freeze but it was the best option to finish her look.

"Don't thank me," Mack said, following Nora out of her room. "Just telling you how it is."

Nora grinned. Mack was right. Genevieve would love her paintings. Everything would go amazingly.

MACK WAS SO, so wrong.

Nora stood frozen as Genevieve strode into the room where Nora kept all of paintings she'd done for the wedding. Genevieve had taken a look at the first painting and her face had shown nothing. She moved onto the second, then the third, and finally got to the sixth. Everything Nora had done so far.

If Genevieve hated it Nora had no idea what she'd do. This represented months of work. She couldn't get everything redone and the other paintings done before the big day. There was no way.

Nora's hands and pits began to sweat. Lovely.

Mack reached for her hand. Nora thought about warning him but before she could say a word about her slick palms Mack had her hand cradled in his. And he acted as if nothing was wrong.

Bless that man.

Genevieve stood in front of that last painting, studying it with critical eyes as she still neither spoke nor showed any kind of emotion.

Would she fire Nora on the spot?

Her stomach curdled even as she willed Genevieve to speak. Anything to end this agony.

"Roger really has such a big head compared to mine," Genevieve finally said. The words were not even close to what Nora had been expecting. "Do you think they can surgically change that?"

Nora glanced up at Mack. They were the only three people in the room so one of them had to respond. But how? Did Genevieve want to grow her own head, or shrink Roger's? Either way Nora doubted that was possible, but then again, Genevieve's world was Hollywood. Who knew?

"I don't think so?" Mack finally said and Nora breathed out a sigh of relief. His answer was the best Nora could have come up with.

"Hm," Genevieve said as she turned back to the painting. "Can you change it here?" she asked Nora.

Nora knew the specific painting Genevieve had pointed out like the back of her hand. It was actually her work in progress so although it wouldn't be an easy fix, she could change the size of Roger's head. Or did Genevieve want her own head changed?

"Roger's head?" Nora asked as hope bloomed within her. If Genevieve was giving her instruction, even if that instruction was a little odd, that meant Nora had done an okay job, right?

Genevieve nodded.

"Of course," Nora replied quickly.

"And I'm glad I saw these. Now I'll make sure to tell the photographer to place us in positions so Roger's head won't look so big. How does he ever get a ball cap on that thing?"

Genevieve asked as she cocked her head while studying said large head in the painting.

Nora shrugged but Genevieve didn't even look her way.

"I'd better get back to my makeup chair. Guests will be arriving soon," Genevieve said as she headed toward the door.

This was it? Her only critique was the size of her fiancé's head? That was good news, right?

"Oh, I forgot to mention. They are stunning, Nora. I love them," Genevieve said as an afterthought right before the door closed behind her, leaving Nora and Mack alone.

"Did she say she loves them?" Nora asked. She turned to Mack, her hands cutting through the air like a crazy person.

But what was one supposed to do with their hands when they were feeling so much?

"She did," Mack said with a giant grin.

"Stunning. She did say stunning, right?" Nora had to make sure she didn't hallucinate and imagine these last two minutes.

"That's what I heard," Mack reassured.

"Oh my heavens!" Nora squealed as she shook her booty and pumped her arms. She surely looked like a mad woman, but at the moment she didn't care.

"I'm not getting fired," Nora said, still dancing ridiculously.

"Not even close," Mack said as he began to laugh. One could only be this close to someone who'd completely lost it for so long before joining in the merriment.

Nora kissed Mack, knowing in the back of her mind it was a bad idea. She had on lipstick that would transfer and they had an entire party to get through before it was just the two of them, but Nora had to kiss her boyfriend. To celebrate with the man who'd never doubted her.

Nora pulled away, rubbing at Mack's lips and getting most of the lipstick off. She hoped the rest wouldn't be noticeable. And if anyone was close enough to Mack to see the tiny bit of lipstick left, good. It would let every woman know that Mack was taken. This was nearly as good as a wedding ring. Maybe Nora should kiss Mack with lipstick on more often.

But her thoughts strayed back to what Genevieve had said. Shrinking Roger's head would be an interesting challenge, but she'd loved them! Hallelujah!

"I have to tell the girls," Nora said, escaping the room with Mack on her heels.

Nora nearly ran down the hall to the ballroom where the party would be. When Nora got to the doorway, she had to pause, the beauty and grandeur stunning her for a few seconds. In one short week, the girls had transformed the place into a garden oasis. They'd had flowers flown in from LA, as nowhere on the island or even in Seattle could gather the blooms Genevieve had demanded in time, but Roger thankfully had a private jet that could get the flowers to Seattle and then the girls had used nearly every employee at the inn, along with their cars, to get the blossoms and greenery from Seattle to the island.

It had been a headache and a half but the final product was beyond compare. Nora wasn't sure how they would top this for Genevieve's wedding. But they would have to.

From the ceiling hung greenery with purple and white flowers woven in. Nora had no idea how the girls had connected the vegetation so seamlessly to the ballroom ceiling. Glowing among the greens and flowers were tiny twinkle lights, giving the room an ethereal atmosphere. Full-grown trees in giant pots were dotted around the room, adding to the fairytale garden ambiance. And they'd blocked off half of the ballroom so the place felt more intimate. It was nearly impossible to tell they were indoors, exactly as Genevieve had wanted.

Round tables were set up all over the room, covered in white and pale green tablecloths. Each table held a huge centerpiece made of the same flowers that hung from the ceiling, but these seemed to grow upwards so it was hard to tell where the ceiling plants ended and the centerpieces began.

But as breathtaking as the room was, Nora wasn't focused on the beauty as she scanned the area with a little frown. There seemed to be no one in the room other than one woman who was setting out gleaming silverware and long-stemmed crystal. The glassware had also been flown in on the private jet. Genevieve had wanted her guests to drink out of one particular type of goblet that was only sold in LA.

"Where are they?" Nora mused to Mack as she backed out of the room and continued down the hall toward the foyer.

It was then that she could hear Elise's voice, calling out commands. Nora realized that Amber was probably in the kitchen with Raul. They'd hired a team to help him, but with a little convincing from Amber, Genevieve had trusted Raul to head the preparation of the entire meal that evening. And since Amber had put her neck on the line, Nora was sure she would stay near the food preparation at all times, just to ensure it all went well.

"The guests will be here in literally fifteen minutes. Why am I having to ask for this vase to be dusted?" Elise shouted, clearly not acting like herself.

"Hey, Sweetie," Nora said as she approached Elise carefully.

With Elise's attention diverted, a young man scurried away, presumably to dust the offending vase.

"Hi, Mama Nora." Elise sounded tired, distracted, and defeated all at once. Poor girl.

"I think we're good, Elise. You two created a vision in that ballroom. Your entryway is always beautiful. It's okay to just take a moment to breathe," Nora said soothingly, trying to calm Elise with her words.

Elise shook her head. "I can breathe when I'm dead."

The fact that Elise didn't even attempt to correct what she'd just said told Nora just how distressed she was.

"As interesting as that sounds, give me this," Nora took a clipboard from Elise's hands.

"Wait! That's my lifeline," Elise said, frantically grasping at it.

"Breathe first, clipboard next." Nora wasn't typically this bossy, especially with Elise. But the poor woman needed an intervention.

Elise took in a quick breath and put out an impatient hand.

"You can do better than that," Nora said with a smile that Elise didn't return. But Nora was sure she would thank her later.

Elise dragged in an exaggerated inhale and spit it out. "Good now?" she asked flatly.

Nora assumed that was as good as it was going to get, so she returned the clipboard.

"Thank you," Elise said with a sigh before looking down at said clipboard. "Everything is checked off," she groaned.

Nora fought a smile. Wasn't checking everything off the goal?

"Meaning you are excellently prepared," Nora said as she ushered Elise upstairs. She knew Elise and Amber had commandeered an empty room for getting ready. Even the short distance to their cottage would be too much to traverse that evening. And although Elise was already in her dress, it was obvious she hadn't really had time to do her hair or makeup.

"Where are we going? I should check in on Genevieve," Elise said, casting an anxious glance down the hall toward the suite where the guest of honor was staying.

"I just saw her. She's fine. You could use some TLC though," Nora tried to say in the most tactful way. Even though

Elise was gorgeous no matter what, the messy bun look just wouldn't fly tonight.

Elise patted her head. "Oh my gosh! I can't believe I forgot to get ready! It wasn't on my list!" Elise tapped an accusing fingernail on her clipboard. "This is like the nightmare I had last night. Mama Nora, we are going to fail!"

Nora worked on hushing Elise as they entered the room, Mack following silently behind. Bless him again.

Amber was exiting the bathroom as they came in. Nora had been wrong. Amber wasn't in the kitchen. But getting ready would have been Nora's next guess if she hadn't been wrapped up in caring for Elise. Unlike Elise, Amber's makeup was perfection and not a hair was out of place.

Her eyes went wide when she saw her sister's state. "Elise!"

"I didn't write down to get ready," Elise pointed at the clipboard once more.

"At least you have your dress on?" Amber said. She spoke in a questioning tone, just as concerned that this was a bad omen.

But Nora knew they had this in hand. "Amber, you start on Elise's face. In five minutes you leave to start greeting guests and Elise can take over on her makeup. I'll use this big blow dryer brush to give you that bouncy hair you love." Nora picked up the device.

"Start," Nora commanded when the other girls seemed frozen.

"Mack, can you look around for Elise's shoes?" Nora asked when she realized Elise was in her tennis shoes. She winced as she scanned the room, which was an absolute disaster of clothing, makeup, and hair products. It would take some digging to find the right shoes.

Mack nodded and Nora hastily slapped products into Elise's hair from the array on the bathroom counter before beginning to blow dry.

Amber and Elise quickly discussed a makeup look and after foundation and concealer were applied Elise went in on her eyes and Amber worked on contour, blush, and highlight.

"I should go," Amber said when her part of the job was done. Six minutes. Pretty dang good.

"We've got this," Nora said over the sound of the blow dryer, feeling even more confident than she had before.

"And I found her shoes," Mack swung a pair of strappy black heels from his finger.

"I'll be there soon," Elise promised Amber, waving her eyeshadow brush.

"Give us ten minutes," Nora added with a nod.

Amber looked unsure as she exited the room but Nora was ready to prove her wrong.

Five minutes later, Nora was letting down the last layer of hair to dry as Elise was applying mascara.

"Oh shoot. Mack! Can you find my earrings?" Elise asked as she held her eyes wide open, swiping upward with the mascara brush.

"What do they look like?" Mack asked, beginning to search before he even heard the answer.

"Silver and dangly," Elise replied.

Mack cringed but just said, "Got it," as he began lifting items of clothing on the dresser.

Nora finished the last layer of hair and began spraying dry shampoo as Elise slipped into her heels. Nora fluffed Elise's hair as Mack cried out triumphantly, "Found them!"

He handed Elise the earrings and she took a quick, critical glance into the mirror.

"A miracle," she mused for a second before rushing to the door.

"Thank you both!" she called behind her, letting the door slam shut.

Nora sank to the bed for a moment. She knew she'd need to get out there soon, but she'd withstood two heart-stopping situations in the last thirty minutes. Her poor knees would give out if they weren't given a break.

"Do you think Genevieve has any idea what she's putting us through?" Nora asked Mack, who leaned against the wall, arms crossed over his chest and biceps straining at the material. Why did the man have to be so danged good-looking? It was distracting.

"Absolutely none," Mack replied with a decisive shake of his head.

Nora thought as much.

She stood, knowing if she didn't she'd make herself comfortable on that bed and never leave. And though she'd survived, maybe even thrived, through Genevieve's evaluation, she still had to attend the party. Amber, Elise, and Genevieve, maybe even Roger, were counting on her.

"Thank you," Nora said as she looked up at Mack, realizing all that he'd already done for her that evening. Not to mention that he'd been so understanding of how little time they were able to spend together in recent days. Even when they had spent time together it was typically doing something for Nora. The man was a saint.

"For what?" Mack asked as if he couldn't fathom what he had done.

"For being here. Searching through this mess of girliness for strappy shoes and dangly earrings. For holding my sweaty hand. For loving me." Nora tried to cover everything, at least all that had happened in the last hour or so.

"Nowhere I'd rather be," Mack said, meeting Nora's eyes unwaveringly.

Nora scoffed.

"Seriously. I want to be with you. You are here, so there's nowhere I'd rather be," Mack reiterated.

Nora felt her heart flip.

"Have I told you how much I love you?" Nora asked and moved as close as she humanly could to Mack.

Mack smirked. "You have. But I like it better when you show me."

Nora laughed. And that was exactly what she planned on doing. She guessed she was going to arrive at the party a little mussed, but she was sure her girls would forgive her.

"MAMA NORA, will you tell Elise that Aiden Christensen won't stop looking at her?" Amber said when Nora and Mack joined them at their table just as dinner was being served. Neither had even seemed to notice that Mack and Nora had arrived a little late.

"Aiden Christensen? Where?" Nora swung her head wildly this way and that to get a view of the heartthrob. Nora wasn't typically the type to get starry-eyed over a celebrity but Aiden Christensen was her exception. The tall, dark, and handsome movie star had played Nora's favorite character of all time, Frederick from the latest movie version of her favorite historical novel. And although Nora was critical about that character with his brooding gaze and broad shoulders, she felt that Aiden Christensen, though young, had portrayed the charming Frederick best of any of the adaptations.

"Mama Nora, play it cool," Elise muttered under her breath. "He's literally right there."

She pointed with her head to the table in front of them.

Nora laid a hand over her heart. "Be still my soul."

"Should I be worried about this?" Mack joked even though he knew full well about Nora's obsession with Frederick.

"Shh," Elise said as other heads at their table began to turn in their direction. Nora wasn't sure who the people were, but after seeing the guest list, she knew the only people on it that weren't the who's who of Hollywood were Nora, Elise, Amber, and Mack.

Nora smiled at their onlookers, who returned a half smile before falling back into conversation. Surely about important things that mere mortals like Nora and her family wouldn't understand.

But as soon as Nora's attention left their tablemates she saw that brooding gaze she'd fallen for onscreen in real life. And Amber was right. It was totally directed at Elise.

"He is," Nora said, surprisingly softly for how excited she was.

Her Elise could marry Frederick!

She knew she was getting way ahead of herself. Elise would be completely annoyed by Nora's thoughts, but this was the best news she'd gotten since . . . well, a little over an hour before when Genevieve had loved her paintings.

"He is not," Elise countered with a shake of her head.

"Then why are you avoiding looking in his direction?" Amber teased because that was exactly what Elise was doing.

"Isn't there somewhere we should be? It seems wrong to just be sitting here." Elise tried to change the topic of conversation.

"There isn't. Because we hired practically an entire second staff to man the party tonight. And we are sitting here because this is exactly where Genevieve wants us to be," Amber said before adding, "so don't try to change the subject. The guy is checking you out and you know it."

Elise glared at her sister and Nora giggled. She loved watching their interaction.

Waiters came around, elegantly placing plates in front of each of them with a detailed explanation of the dish. Nora looked down to see a single tiny cracker, apparently handmade in an Austrian village, with an equally small piece of smoked wild salmon caught and numbered in Alaska, topped with caviar straight from Russia. Nora wasn't sure she was going to like the proportions of the dish but wasn't about to say anything aloud. Not when her daughter's fiancé was the chef.

Nora waited to see how the fancy people at their table ate it and when they took their forks and popped the whole thing into their mouths at once, Nora followed suit.

"Yum," she said appreciatively. She wasn't even a huge caviar fan and that had been delicious.

Amber beamed with pride for Raul and Nora fought between feeling pleased that her daughter was so happy to worrying for her the way she did anytime she thought about Amber and Raul. Nora wanted to feel nothing but excitement for their upcoming nuptials but she still wasn't sure about Raul. Amber had so much to lose with the union and Raul had every-thing to gain. But Nora just crossed her fingers that Raul really was in love.

Elise had told Nora she was going to broach the conversa-tion of a prenup one more time. She said she wasn't worried about her part in the inn—if Amber lost Elise would lose right alongside of her—and Nora agreed. She was fine with not getting a return on her investment in the inn, she just wanted Amber protected. So Elise was going to try. Assuming the right opportunity came along.

"I think I'm going to check in on the kitchen," Amber said, standing.

"I knew you had somewhere to be," Elise muttered.

But Amber just laughed because with her movement Aiden wasn't just glancing in their direction; he'd turned his whole body to see what was going on. And although he glanced at Amber for a split second, his attention went right back to Elise.

"Make sure she gives him her number," Amber instructed Nora before leaving the table.

"I don't have to make sure that happens, do I?" Nora asked Elise, scooting over to take Amber's empty seat.

"He's not going to ask me for my number," Elise said with a wave of her hand.

"But what if he does?" Nora asked.

"What if the sky falls?" Elise retorted, looking exasperated.

Mack snorted.

Nora turned to scowl at him.

"It's a valid question," he said with a shrug and Nora couldn't help but smile at Mack's cuteness.

"I just realized, though: we need to throw one of these for Amber, don't we?" Elise said, still seeming to look for a change of topic. But this time Nora was swayed because Elise was right. They did need to throw a shower for Amber.

"Not quite on this scale, but yeah," Nora agreed. She'd forgotten about this tradition. Which was strange, considering they were literally in the process of throwing one for Genevieve, but Nora had a feeling they were all still hoping the actual wedding day wouldn't come. And because of that, it wasn't surprising they might forget about a wedding shower.

"I talked to her about the prenup," Elise said softly, her thoughts seeming to be along the same lines as Nora's.

"And?" Nora asked.

Mack moved into Nora's old seat so that he could hear the conversation over the sound of the harp playing several feet away.

"She didn't get mad but she said she wasn't going to do it. Kept saying it wasn't the foot she wanted to start a marriage on."

Nora understood that. Typically she'd applaud that. But

with Raul, Nora wanted Amber to be extra careful. Maybe he wasn't using her at all, yet some things about their relationship just felt a little off. But then again, being the overprotective sister and mom that Elise and Nora were, maybe they were seeing things that weren't there? Nora could hope. Because for better or worse this wedding seemed to be happening.

"So we plan a shower," Nora said resolutely.

"And a wedding," Elise added.

Nora nodded. It was all they could do.

But she brightened up when a certain dark-haired gentleman turned his eyes toward Elise once again.

"He's not looking at me," Elise said before Nora could say anything.

"I respectfully disagree," Nora replied.

"I even have to side with Nora on this one. Dude isn't being subtle in the least," Mack added.

"Ha!" Nora said triumphantly, her eyes wide with victory.

Elise rolled her eyes. "Even if he is looking, it doesn't mean anything. Guys like that look at women all the time. It means nothing."

But Nora hardly heard a word she said because Aiden had stood. And Nora swore he was still looking Elise's way as he did so.

"He's standing," Nora whispered urgently as Elise shushed her. Nora knew Elise was right and she had to play it cool so she worked hard to school her features but he was walking their direction!

Nora hastily pushed Mack back to his old seat and slid over to hers. She was sure Aiden saw the exchange but didn't care. Either he'd walk right past them or he'd be grateful to Nora for leaving the seat next to his potential lady love open. Oh heavens, Frederick would feel gratitude toward her!

Nora worked hard not to hyperventilate as Aiden stopped

behind the open seat Nora had just left. "Would it be alright if I sat here for a minute?" he asked graciously.

Nora bit her lip to keep from saying anything embarrassing.

"Actually, my sister is just up seeing that everything is okay in the kitchen. She'll be back any second," Elise practically lied. Who knew when Amber would be back?

"She could also be gone for a while," Nora countered. She wasn't going to let poor Aiden fall prey to a lie.

"We don't know that," Elise said to Nora.

Nora subtly tried to nod in the direction of Aiden. Elise was all but ignoring the man who still stood.

"Well, when she comes back I'll gladly return her seat," Aiden offered gallantly. Nora knew he'd be just like Frederick.

Elise finally looked up at Aiden and lifted one shoulder. "Then have a seat."

It sounded as if she was being asked to fill in for someone getting a root canal, not having one of the most gorgeous men on the planet ask if he could sit next to her.

"Elise," Nora mouthed when Elise looked at her, hoping it would remind the girl to be on her best behavior.

"I'm Aiden." He offered his hand and a polite introduction toward Mack. That was nice of him to include Mack.

"Mack." Mack took Aiden's hand and shook it before offering it to Nora.

Nora felt her cheeks pink as she tried to tell herself this wasn't Frederick in the flesh, but it sure felt like it was. It was also a little weird to watch her real-life boyfriend meet her fictional crush.

It took all of Nora's willpower not to flutter her eyelashes as she introduced herself. Thankfully Aiden moved on to Elise.

"Elise," she said as she barely touched his hand and then let go.

"Nice to meet you all," he said graciously.

Mack and Nora returned pleasantries but Elise just offered a tight smile. What was with her?

"So how do you all know Genevieve and Roger?" Aiden asked, a bit of his southern twang coming through as he spoke. Nora might have watched the true Hollywood story on Aiden's life and knew he'd grown up splitting time between his dad in Texas and his mom and sisters in Oklahoma.

"We're the help," Elise said. "That's why my sister went to check on the kitchen. We weren't invited; we're working the event."

"Event planners? My sister plans weddings back in Oklahoma," Aiden said with about as much charm as Nora had ever witnessed. And to turn that on in the face of Elise's coldness? The man was good.

"They do that. But they also own this inn." Nora had to brag about her girls, since evidently Elise was unwilling to do so for herself.

"Really?" Aiden asked. "The whole property is stunning."

"It wasn't that way when they bought it. You should see the befores and afters on this place," Nora said.

"I'd love to." Aiden's smile grew as Elise glared at Nora from behind Aiden.

Nora pretended she couldn't see her. Elise would thank her one day.

"Elise would love to show you," Nora continued as Elise's scowl deepened.

Nora fought hard not to laugh. Even angry Elise was adorable.

"How do you know Genevieve and Roger?" Elise asked, obviously trying to move the conversation along so she wouldn't have to commit to showing Aiden the photos. Elise's scowl was a little less noticeable when Aiden turned back to speak to her.

"I work with Roger," Aiden said modestly. No mentions of

the movies that Roger had produced and Aiden had starred in. Nope, just that they work together. This guy was about as opposite from the Hollywood stereotype as Nora could imagine. Well, besides his extreme good looks and his charm. Why wouldn't Elise give him a shot?

Even the fancy pants sitting across from them seemed enraptured in all that Aiden had to say. They'd started paying attention to the lowly side of the table as soon as Aiden had filled the empty seat.

"That's nice," was all Elise said and Nora could see she was about to close the conversation.

"I'd better get back to my table," Aiden said, standing in the nick of time before Elise dismissed him. "But Elise, can I get your number? That way we can set up a time for me to see those pictures Nora promised."

Oh, he was good. Nora would applaud him if she didn't think it would hurt his chances to get Elise's number. Although if Elise didn't give it to him, Nora just might.

"My sister and I would be happy to show them to you," Elise said in an overly sweet manner that wouldn't have her winning any Oscars.

"I'd love that."

Aiden stood waiting.

Elise sighed softly.

"It's 555-712-1284," she finally said.

Aiden grinned even though he made no move to put it into his phone, surprising Nora. Had it all been an act? Why wouldn't he take down the number he'd been given?

But Elise seemed pleased by the turn of events, even going so far as to return Aiden's grin.

"See ya, Aiden," she said happily, probably feeling that Aiden had just proved her point. He didn't actually want her number. He just wanted to show that he could get it.

"See you soon, Elise," Aiden countered.

It was like watching a movie! But what about the number?

Aiden walked away and Elise turned back to Nora and Mack. The fancy pants all went back to their own conversations.

"And I guess I'll never be hearing from Aiden Christensen again," Elise said with a smirk as her phone chimed.

She pulled it out and Nora read over her shoulder.

Lovely chatting with you, Elise. I'm up for picture gazing anytime. Let me know when you're free.

Nora sat in amazement as Elise seemed frozen in shock. He'd memorized her number. The guy was better than any of them could have ever imagined. Elise finally shook herself out of it. "Why pursue this?" she asked. "I live here. He lives in LA. There is no point."

"It looks like Aiden disagrees," Mack said with a nod in the direction of where Aiden sat.

Sure enough, the man had a grin on his face that on anyone else would look plain goofy. On Aiden it was delightful.

Elise tucked her phone away. "I'll just ignore him for the evening. He'll forget all about me when he flies home tonight."

Elise's phone chimed again.

Oh, and I should have complimented your suites during our conversation. I loved mine at first sight when I checked in. I can't wait to stay the night. And honestly, with how much I've enjoyed the island so far, I might just stay longer.

"Ugh," Elise groaned but before she glanced down Nora saw what she'd been trying to hide. A smile played at the corners of Elise's lips. She had been pleasantly surprised by Aiden. He wasn't who she'd expected. He'd still have work to do but Nora guessed he would one day win Elise over.

And Nora would have Frederick as a son-in-law.

"IT'S JUST A SHORT HIKE," Julia promised her mom and her sister.

After six days together, with mostly just the three of them because Wendy had had to work more often than not and she went back to her own apartment every night, Julia needed to get outside. She didn't care if it was a brisk fifty degrees—they'd all grown up in the Midwest and had been outside for long periods of time in much worse—she needed to get out of the house and into nature.

And this nature walk that some considered a hike would be perfect for all of them, even her septuagenarian mother. Betty, despite her helpless act, was in fantastic shape.

"But it's October," Lacey protested as she looked out at the gray day with a grimace.

Typically gray days didn't bother Julia, but being stuck in the house for a week with her family during such weather wasn't good for her mental health. Even though her sister and mother had improved since their arrival, no longer criticizing and complaining with every other sentence (just every fourth or fifth sentence), Julia needed a break. And fresh air would give that break she desperately craved.

"I don't do hikes, Julia," Betty said with finality from where she sat at a table in the breakfast nook.

Lacey was leaning on the kitchen counter, drinking her protein shake as they spoke.

Though they were definitely driving her up the wall, Julia smiled at the scene before her. Her mom and sister were comfortable in her home. Just a couple of years before she wouldn't have believed it was possible. So even though they still didn't see eye-to-eye and sometimes they made her question her sanity, her relationship with her family was improving and Julia would take that.

Julia looked to Lacey. There was no way of convincing Betty to do something when she got that tone.

"Lace?" Julia heard the desperation in her tone. Would her sister hear it too? Would that cause her to dig in her heels or to feel some pity for her? Julia wasn't sure but she figured she was about to find out.

"It's short?" Lacey asked.

Julia nodded.

"And we'll go into town afterward? Around the time Wendy has her lunch break?"

Julia nodded fervently. She knew getting to see Wendy would be a motivating factor.

"Fine," Lacey conceded before downing the last of her shake.

Julia couldn't help her giant grin.

"Yes, you two go. Don't worry about leaving me behind," Betty said with a wave of her hand, her tone telling Julia she very much should worry about leaving her mother behind, but Julia didn't acknowledge it.

Not when she was so close to a taste of freedom.

Lacey was already in workout clothes. Although she was reluctant to admit it to Julia, she'd been loving Julia's home gym each morning.

Julia was dressed for the hike as well so they found a couple of jackets and were off in Julia's cute sports coupe within minutes.

"Do you remember when we did the Travers Family Run Day?" Lacey asked as Julia drove down the hills around her home to get to Elliot Drive, which would take them around the island to the base of the "hike."

"Oh my gosh, yes," Julia managed before she fell into laughter.

She must have been eight years old, maybe nine. Her brother Jack had been just getting into running—he'd been a sports star for years, but had decided he was now going to rule the track. Somehow he'd convinced beauty queen Lacey to join them and all five Prices had shown up at that starting line at 8am on a Saturday morning. To say their father wasn't a morning person would be putting it lightly. Julia had only ever seen her dad awake before noon for work or if Jack had a sports game of some sort. Julia was pretty sure Jack had only been able to convince Dad because it was for the good of a sport that they do this race.

But at that starting line it was as if some part of their morning-hating father had awakened, realizing he had no obligation to be there. He'd scowled and when the race began he refused to run with the rest of the crowd, standing stock still in the middle of the street and making them all run around him.

Because Betty wouldn't go without her husband, she stood by his side. Jack had left them long behind, realizing his family would just slow him down in his goal of beating Peter

McConkie's time. Julia still wasn't sure why they'd all been invited. Maybe because Peter's family was running?

Lacey had been red-cheeked and devastated, sure that her chances at whatever crown she was working toward in that moment were ruined by her father's unwillingness to fulfil his civic duty of moving when in the middle of a race.

After Julia had seen that her father was in no real danger, she had thought it all quite interesting, one of her better mornings in Travers. Especially when they'd all ended up at Merv's for late morning shakes and burgers.

"I thought Dad was going to get trampled," Julia finally managed between her laughter.

"Mom would never have allowed that," Lacey said matter-of-factly, causing Julia to laugh even harder because she was right. If Mom put her mind to anything, it would happen. Even parting the crowds during a race. "I was much more worried about my dreams for that crown."

Julia nodded as her laughter abated. Lacey's life had always revolved around seeking that next crown.

"Was it hard for you?" Julia asked, thinking about the end of her own career. It had been rough but the time had been right. Lacey had had to give up her pageant dreams after getting pregnant with Trip. Sure, she could have run for Mrs. Something or other, but that wasn't really Lacey's style.

"When my pageant days came to an end?" Lacey asked for clarification.

Julia nodded, her eyes on the road. The car in front of her had to be a tourist with the way they were cruising down the coast so slowly.

"I guess it was? I'm not even sure I thought about it much. I was supposed to compete in pageants until I caught myself a husband. That had always been the plan. Then have babies and now this." Lacey held a hand out toward the ocean.

"Looking at the ocean?" Julia asked.

Lacey shook her head. "Chasing my baby halfway across the country," she said before biting her lip.

They drove in silence for a few minutes, Julia deep in her own thoughts just as surely as Lacey was in hers. Julia knew it had been hard on Lacey when Julia left. When Wendy, her only daughter, took that same path it had to have nearly devastated her change-hating, status-quo-loving sister.

"This isn't a dig, I promise." Lacey broke the silence.

Julia tensed. It didn't sound like this would be complimentary.

"But until you have a child of your own, you'll never understand this kind of pain. Travers was all I ever wanted. I get that it wasn't the same for you, but to have your baby girl, to whom you tried to give everything, decide it wasn't enough for her? It made me even more mad at you to think of the hurt you caused Mom."

Julia nodded once. If she tried, it was easy enough to wrap her mind around Lacey's explanation. Julia had no idea what it was like to be left behind. She knew what it was like to be so trapped in a town that she felt like she literally wouldn't survive another minute, that she wouldn't be able to breathe again until she left, but being the one watching her go? She hadn't experienced that and Julia could imagine that it would be a kind of hurt she couldn't comprehend.

And Betty and Lacey had experienced it twice.

"You might think that all that yelling you've done since you came back to Travers hasn't sunk into this hard skull of mine, but it has. I've heard you. I get that you felt like you had to go. I don't understand it, but I believe that's what you felt. But have you tried to think about what it was like for me and mom?" Lacey asked Julia.

Had she? Maybe in passing, but had she ever really tried to

imagine that kind of pain? It was hard for Julia to imagine being the one left—with her personality she would have jumped up to go with whoever was doing the leaving—but she tried to imagine if she'd been like Lacey. All of her hopes and dreams had been fulfilled in Travers. And then to have someone she loved so much not just leave but seem to turn her back on everything you deemed important? Yeah, that wouldn't feel good.

"I am now," Julia said as she pulled into a parking spot close to the trailhead. Fall wildflowers bloomed all around them.

Lacey opened her door and Julia followed suit. They began walking the slightly uphill trek as Julia spoke once more, "I should have done it before. I'm not so good with empathy."

Lacey grunted. "None of us Prices are. Why do you think we can hold onto grudges for decades? Anyone with a pinky full of empathy can't be that stubborn." Lacey winked and suddenly Julia was transported back to a time when she'd idolized everything about her big sister. Julia had wanted to win every pageant, to be the town's darling, just because it was what Lacey had done. Lacey would wink and the town would cheer.

And in her own way Julia had accomplished following in her sister's footsteps. Just on a slightly bigger stage.

"You seem less angry with me now," Julia ventured to say. She might get her head bitten off for her comment but she had to see if Lacey was open to more of a relationship with Julia. As much as Julia liked to think herself independent she'd love to have a true bond with her sister once more.

Lacey nodded as she skirted a fallen tree branch.

The forest just next to this part of Elliot Drive was gorgeous, full of giant trees and lush undergrowth. There were plenty of trails back here, one leading to the inn Amber and Elise had remodeled. The one Julia and Lacey traversed was a lot more used than that one, especially when tourists and locals came back here in droves during the summer. But on a fall day like today even this trail was pretty quiet; while Julia had seen a couple of cars in the lot at the base of the trail, they had yet to see other hikers. Granted, they had just started.

"Trip and I had an argument about Wendy. He was sure I was coming on this trip to bring her home. I asked him how on earth he thought I was supposed to do that. He said tell her she had to, if she wanted to be a part of this family. He sounded so much like me at that age I was kind of shocked. When I got over it, I told him that it wasn't fair to ask that of Wendy. That we needed to love her no matter her choices. He wasn't too pleased with my reaction and stormed off to his girlfriend's house. She's a good Travers girl and he'll probably wind up making her his wife in the next year or so. Anyway, he left me alone with my thoughts, in my house I loved so much, surrounded by neighbors who made me feel comfortable, in a town I knew like the back of my hand. It was my place. My safety and security. But I then began to imagine what it had looked like to Wendy. The chipping paint in our kitchen as well as on half of the town. The long winters and the hot and sometimes unbearably humid summers. What I saw as quaint she could see as beyond its prime. What I saw as comfortable, she called boring. Why would I want my baby girl to stay in town just to make me happy?"

Lacey had stayed in front of Julia, keeping her face forward, so Julia had no idea what her sister's expression was. Julia wasn't sure how to respond . . . should she respond? Because she was nearly speechless. Lacey really had taken the time to see things from her point of view. Well, it was really from Wendy's point of view, but it was close enough. That description of Travers explained exactly what Julia had felt. And she'd been wracked with guilt for years for having those feelings.

"I wouldn't," Lacey said, answering her own question. "And then it hit me hard. I wouldn't have wanted you to stay either. It just hurt that I didn't seem to know any of what you felt beforehand. You seemed just fine one minute and the next you were gone."

"I wasn't sure how to talk to you about what I felt," Julia said honestly. Back then she'd tried to tell her sister in roundabout ways how miserable she was in Travers, but Lacey seemed to hear only what she wanted to.

Granted, most people in their late teens and early twenties would have done the same. It was a selfish time in life, which was normal considering all of the big life decisions many made during that time, but it wasn't great for relationships.

"Or you might have tried and I just wouldn't listen. I couldn't have imagined a life without you back then, Jules," Lacey said, her speed ramping up with each emotion-filled word. "And to feel that way but then have you leave? It was like you were fine without us, without me. While I barely managed to go on. Mom sometimes had to drag me out of bed. It went on like that for months. You broke my heart, Julia."

Julia felt tears streaming down her cheeks. She'd not known. Not that she had asked. She'd been so consumed with her own situation she didn't have the bandwidth to worry about anyone else, even her own sister.

"And then you came back to town years later and it felt like moments later Wendy began talking about leaving town too. I didn't think I'd survive being left behind twice."

Julia nodded. She wanted to say something but the lump in her throat kept her from voicing her thoughts. Not that she had many. She just felt so sorry.

"But I did. We all did," Lacey said, her voice cracking. Julia could tell her sister was crying as well but they both worked hard to hide it. It was the Price way.

"I'm sorry," Julia finally managed.

Lacey waved her apology away. "You shouldn't have to be. You were living your life. As your loving sister, I should have encouraged you. I was selfish."

"So was I," Julia said as she wiped at her eyes. She could see the end of the trail coming up and she didn't want Lacey to see how much she'd been crying.

"Imagine that. The Price girls acting selfishly. I feel like this is why Paster Rob tried to get us to do more service back in Sunday School."

Julia chuckled. Poor Pastor Rob and his attempt at making the Price girls less self-centered and vain. It had taken them close to forty years after his lessons to finally start down that path.

"Do you want to start over?" Lacey asked in a tremulous voice.

Julia froze. She literally could not take another step. What had Lacey offered?

"Really?" Julia asked when she got over her shock.

Lacey turned around and nodded. "I'm sick of the way things are."

"Me too," Julia agreed immediately.

"I can't promise to be less critical."

"I can't promise not to take offense."

"But I can promise I'll try to apologize."

"And I'll try to accept your apology."

Julia realized she and Lacey were finally recognizing their own faults instead of the other's.

Lacey stuck out her hand and Julia immediately grasped it, finishing the handshake with a tight squeeze.

Julia grinned and Lacey's own wide smile matched it.

"This means you'll sometimes stay in *my* guest room when you come to visit Travers. Instead of always staying at Mom's,"

Lacey said with a raised eyebrow.

"In the house with chipping paint in the kitchen?" Julia spoke in her best diva voice as she pressed her hand to her chest as if she couldn't imagine doing such a thing.

"Oh, shut it," Lacey remarked.

Julia laughed. "I'll love every minute of it."

"Don't you start lying now. We know we'll drive one another to the brink of insanity. But that's what family does."

"At least our family," Julia amended.

Lacey chuckled as she nodded in agreement. Julia couldn't help but join in her laughter.

The sisters headed back down the trail, a family of four passing them. The two daughters kept casting strange looks back at Julia and Lacey as their laughter continued for far too long.

"And I won't oppose you flying me out here first class every few months," Lacey said once their laughter finally calmed.

Julia nearly leaped for joy but decided to play it cool. That was what Lacey would appreciate.

"Does that mean you'll have to stay at my house?" Julia asked as if she was put out by that fact.

"Unless your rich boyfriend wants to let me stay at his place while he's on tour?"

Julia laughed again. "You wish. A mansion to yourself would be your dream. You are stuck with me, sister."

Lacey looped an arm through Julia's as the two continued toward the car. She then let go of Julia to yank off her jacket.

"You should have warned me it would get hot as we hiked," Lacey said, causing Julia's feathers to ruffle.

And she was already back to complaining. Was this the same woman who'd been worried it would be too cold to leave the house? The woman who lived in freezing temperatures for a good couple months a year, and yet was blaming this on Julia?

But suddenly her ruffled feathers smoothed. She and Lacey were trying to make things work. They'd have good days and bad days and she knew that some things would never change and she was okay with that. This was her sister. And Julia loved her, all of her, for better or worse.

CHAPTER FOURTEEN

PIPER HAD THOUGHT LONG and hard over where to come today. Well, not too long and hard, considering she'd only agreed to remarry Carter a week before, but she'd taken some time and lots of thought.

She wanted to be in a place where she'd feel Kristie. It felt wrong that her baby girl wasn't with them on this day that Kristie had dreamed of for so long. The one she'd put into motion even while knowing her death would rob her of seeing her parents' happiness.

Because Piper *was* happy, sometimes blissfully so. There was still a raincloud that would form overhead, sometimes for minutes, other times for hours or even days, but she was learning tactics for dispelling that cloud. Sometimes a funny memory of Kristie worked; sometimes it only helped to darken the cloud and keep it around for longer. Grief was a beast. But it was also a beast that could be tamed. As much as Piper hated to admit it, time was a healer. It didn't heal all of her wounds, but she didn't want them all healed. To no longer feel pain seemed like it would mean she no longer cared and loved. And she would forever and ever love her daughter.

Piper's mom worried that Kristie's final wish was the only reason Piper was marrying Carter again. Her parents had seen the hurt Carter had caused; they'd been there to help Piper pick up the pieces after he'd left. But they'd only seen a minimal amount of the way he'd been there for her and Kristie during Kristie's illness and then just for Piper in those dark days following Kristie's death.

And as Piper considered her mom's concern she realized that maybe she was remarrying Carter because of Kristie. But not in the way her mother worried. Yes, it had been Kristie's last hope that her parents reunite, but that wasn't the true reason Piper had chosen Carter. Piper was giving him this second chance—giving *them* this second chance—because of the way he'd stepped up and proved himself. And he may have never been given that opportunity were it not for Kristie. It was because of her illness, her time of need and therefore Piper's time of need, that there had been the time and space for Carter to step back into their lives and prove himself. Not that Piper was grateful for Kristie's cancer, but if they'd had to endure it, if she had to lose her baby girl, at least something good had come out of the most terrible thing that had ever happened to her.

"You can still back out," said Piper's father, Randall, as he drove Piper and her mother in Piper's little black sedan.

"Dad," Piper warned. Both of her parents had promised to be on their best behavior today. Not that she blamed them for their hurt. They'd loved Carter too, so when he left it had broken all of their hearts. It had also broken their trust in the man who had once promised to always care for Piper and Kristie. But what they didn't quite know, because they hadn't seen it firsthand, was that Carter had come back to fulfill that promise and then some. While her parents still might not trust Carter, Piper realized that she did. Completely.

"Just pointing out your options," Randall said as he glanced into the rearview mirror to the backseat where Piper sat alone.

She was alone for the moment, but the alone portion of her life was almost over. She bit her lip in anticipation. They'd be meeting with up with Carter as well as Reverend Hammond and Carter's parents soon.

"I think it's too late for that now," Mitzi said with a fond smile as she turned to look at Piper. "She has the glow of a woman in love."

Piper smiled, peace overcoming her. To others it may not have seemed like much but Piper knew her mother. Those words had been her mom's way of saying she approved. And even though Piper would have gotten married without her mom's approval, as she knew this was the right thing for her, she was glad to have it. Although it looked like Carter would still have to prove himself to Randall.

But even if her father wasn't fully on board with everything, Piper couldn't be more grateful for her parents. Other than Carter, they'd been the ones who had walked with her every step of the way. They'd seen her grief and tried to lift her. Even that morning as Piper had gotten ready they'd helped to clean and move things around in Piper's home to make room for Carter. He'd be coming home with her after the wedding and the next day, in lieu of a honeymoon, the two had decided to move Carter from his apartment into the home they'd once shared. That was Piper's version of romance.

"She does look beautiful," Randall said grudgingly as if he couldn't help but admit it.

Piper looked at her lap that was covered by the gray lace that overlaid her white slip dress. The dress had been a difficult decision. With only a week to prep Piper knew she should find something already on the island. She'd gone to a few boutiques that had white dresses and nothing felt right. At the final store she saw this gray lace dress. The lace created a beautiful design of flowers and underneath the lace was a plain white satin dress that went down to her feet. The sleeves were long and ended in bells while the rest was rather figure-hugging. When Piper tried it on she couldn't help but think of the term 'half mourning' that she'd often read in regency romance novels. She knew it was a time when one no longer wore black, instead opting for soft colors like lavender and gray. And although that might seem morbid, this wedding was helping Piper to move on to half mourning. She would still grieve deeply some days but with the joy of moving forward with Carter she would no longer dwell on that pain each and every moment.

Her mom hadn't been thrilled with the choice of a gray dress but Piper couldn't leave it after she thought of that term. And it looked pretty fantastic on her petite frame against her blond hair, if she did say so herself.

"Thanks Dad," Piper responded, a smile on her lips.

She was marrying Carter. Again.

It wasn't hard to conjure up memories of her first wedding day, their first wedding day. Piper had been so nervous she'd hardly eaten anything in the twenty-four hours before. Between that and the fact that her white dress had had a corset, she worked hard to keep from fainting all day. Thankfully her work paid off and she'd stayed upright for the ceremony and reception.

This time was so different. Piper had enjoyed a breakfast of eggs and toast as well as a midmorning snack of apples and peanut butter. Her stomach was at ease along with the rest of her. Nerves weren't her companion at all. Just joy, peace, and satisfaction. This was the right thing. She felt it so deep in her soul she couldn't have put the feeling there herself.

"I'm just not sure what's the big hurry. Didn't you just get engaged last week?" her dad muttered.

Piper smiled. Her father was a bit of a grump but he was their grump. And Piper loved him for it. If he wasn't muttering or cursing he wouldn't be her dad.

Carter and Piper had considered a longer engagement period, planning a big party, but the more Piper thought about that, the more she was against it. She had at first wanted it to be just her and Carter. But then she realized they needed someone to marry them, along with two witnesses, and she knew if she chose anyone other than her parents to be those witnesses they'd be deeply hurt.

So Piper had approached Carter with the idea of getting married right away with just six in attendance, along with Reverend Hammond who'd helped them through not only Kristie's death but a lot of her life as well.

"I love it," Carter had immediately responded before kissing Piper.

Piper was pretty sure she could have said just about anything and gotten that reaction, but with Carter on board, they'd moved forward quickly and the day had finally come.

Piper thought 'finally' because it was a long time in the making, even if the engagement was short. She and Carter had been lost for far too long. This was the start of them being found —they'd found each other, but Piper had also found herself once more. A new version of herself. That didn't mean she loved Kristie any less; it just meant she was learning how to cope with her new future.

Her dad eased the car into a space next to the beach. Their beach.

Piper had considered a number of wedding locales. One of Kristie's favorite parks, the courthouse, the church where she and Carter were first married, even Las Vegas, but nothing had felt as right as this spot. Not only had it been a favorite for their family, but it was sentimental for Carter and Piper. The perfect place for their new beginning.

After her dad parked, Piper's eyes immediately began scouring the shoreline in search of one person. And there he stood, not far from the road, the ocean at his back as he searched just as fiercely for Piper.

Their eyes met and Piper couldn't help but laugh. Neither had known what the other was going to wear that day, yet there Carter stood, in a gray suit with a white flower in his lapel. They couldn't have matched any better if they'd tried.

Piper flung open her car door before Carter or her dad could reach it to open it for her and jumped out, eager to get the show in the road. The wind whipped at her simple French twist and she could feel strands escape but she couldn't care less. She was on a beautiful beach marrying the love of her life.

"You are breathtaking," Carter said softly. His long legs had eaten up the distance between them in seconds.

He took both of her hands in his and Piper beamed. She'd never felt more beautiful in her life.

"You clean up quite nicely yourself," Piper said, beaming so intensely her cheeks hurt but she just couldn't help it.

Carter then tucked Piper under his arm to shelter her from the wind as best he could. She could feel his attention move to her parents, who had also gotten out of the car.

"Sir," Carter said, nodding to Randall and putting out a hand.

Randall eyed the hand for a moment. "Promise you'll take better care of her heart this time."

Carter gave a single nod, knowing he deserved the admonition. "The best," he promised both Randall and Piper.

"Good. That's what she deserves." Randall cleared his throat to cover up the fact that he was choking up and turned to

Mitzi, the only person Piper's dad ever turned to when his emotions overcame him. She knew to simply pat his arm.

Piper knew that if he could, her dad would have shielded her from all of the world's hurts. The fact that Piper had experienced so many had wounded her father in a way nothing else could have.

"Do you want to walk her to the Reverend?" Carter offered Piper's dad even as neither Carter nor Piper moved. Piper was quite enjoying this spot safe against Carter's body.

"I think it's your job to walk with her now," Randall said firmly.

Piper loved that. And it was the truth. She and Carter hadn't made their vows this time around yet, but it was their job to walk together, side by side.

So Carter led her to where the reverend stood by a large rock that would shield them from some of the fierce winds. Piper knew she should be cold. She saw her mom shivering, and even her dad had his arms crossed over his chest in an attempt to keep warm, but Piper felt none of it. Maybe because she was still tucked into Carter's side or maybe because she was high on bliss.

Piper and Carter stopped in front of Reverend Hammond, the latter giving Piper a wink. He'd seen so much of Piper's sorrow as well. She could imagine he was rejoicing with her today.

Piper only left the cocoon of Carter to turn to her former and future in-laws. Carter's father gave Piper a welcoming hug while his mother added a kiss to her greeting before pushing her right back into Carter's arms.

The ceremony was a quick one; they'd wanted it that way. The reverend said the words he had to and before they knew it Carter and Piper were kissing, a chaste kiss that was pastor and parent appropriate. But unlike the first time they did this, this time Piper knew what the evening had in store for her and her core warmed.

Being with Carter in every way was exquisite. Piper couldn't believe she had him back in her life like this . . . forever.

But those thoughts were pushed aside for the time being. She was still standing in front of the reverend, after all.

Once the minister left, the parents began to discuss where to go to dinner to celebrate. They'd always gotten along well, even while Carter and Piper had been divorced.

Piper felt a sudden burst of joy, realizing she was no longer divorced from Carter.

She thought of the days of pain and bitterness she'd endured when he'd first left. She would never, ever have believed they would be here, that she could have not only forgiven Carter but learned to trust him, and couldn't help but love him again.

"Do you want to go to dinner?" Carter interrupted her thoughts.

Boy, did she love him. So much. With every fiber of her being.

Piper shook her head.

Carter grinned.

"You all go on without us," he told the others as he and Piper backed away from the group discussion.

"What?" Mitzi asked.

Carter's dad laughed.

Piper took that as permission and began running to Carter's car, a feeling of wild abandon making her a little reckless. Carter's laughter followed her and she heard him close on her heels before he caught up with her, taking her hand and running down the hard sand of the beach, ruining their outfits forever.

But Piper wouldn't have traded that moment for a thousand beautiful dresses.

Piper slowed down as they reached the car, laughter spilling out of her when she could finally breathe again.

Suddenly she was off her feet, swept up into Carter's arms.

"You're supposed to carry me over the threshold," Piper reprimanded even as she delighted in her circumstances.

"Oh, I'll be doing that too," Carter promised as he somehow managed to open the passenger's door and gently deposit Piper onto the front seat.

He ran around the car and jumped in the driver's seat.

"Where to?" he asked, his face alight with his grin. Piper had always loved that smile and now it was hers again.

"Are you hungry?" she asked.

"Not really," Carter said, his smile morphing into something sexier.

"Home?" Piper asked as her stomach flipped in anticipation.

"Our home," Carter said as if he couldn't quite believe they shared a home once more.

And with that Piper made a silent vow to them both. Things would come that would try to break them. Last time she'd allowed them to be broken, she'd let Carter leave on his own even though he'd wanted her with him. From now on, she promised, she would always choose him. Carter over everything. She would pick them.

CHAPTER FIFTEEN

"HEY, MAMA NORA?" Amber said as she poked her head into Nora's makeshift workspace.

Nora looked away from the canvas at hand to turn her attention to her daughter.

"I have a question for you if you have some time?" Amber asked as she stepped into the room, closing the door behind her.

"Of course." Nora set down her paintbrush. There was something about Amber's tone, the way she'd walked in and asked for Nora's attention, that told Nora this was important. She needed to treat it as such.

"Do you agree with my family?" Amber asked as she leaned on the door behind her. "Do you think I should get a prenuptial agreement before marrying Raul?"

Oh heavens. This Nora had not been expecting. She wished she had been because then she could have been ready with the right answer. She really didn't want to mess this up.

Nora had actually spent much of the last few weeks worried about Amber and Raul. Their wedding was approaching in just a couple of short weeks and Nora wondered if Raul would really become her son-in-law. Part of her had thought it impossible. The man just didn't seem worthy of her daughter. Nora couldn't put her finger on it, but with the way he only seemed to attend to her when he had to, he just didn't have the glow about him that a man truly in love should. Yes, he was charming; yes, he said all of the right things; but there was something just beyond the tangible that felt off. But the other part of her had to acknowledge that it was inevitable. The engagement was official, the wedding was practically already planned and it didn't seem that Amber felt the same way the rest of them did. She was in love. And she trusted in the man she had chosen.

"I think—" Nora needed more time to think on this. But she didn't have it. She sent up the quickest prayer for guidance and opened her mouth to speak again. "You should think about your reasons for not wanting to get one."

That was not what Nora had been planning on saying but when the thought came to her it had felt right so she went with it. Now she wondered if she'd said the right thing.

"I have been. A lot," Amber confided as she tapped on the door she leaned against.

"And?" Nora asked, prompting her daughter for more information.

"It boils down to what I've been saying. I don't want to start my marriage on the wrong foot by demanding a paper be signed in case we break up. It's not a future I ever even want to imagine."

Nora noticed that Amber hadn't said it was an impossible future. So many in her shoes would have. Nora would venture to guess that there was something about Raul that was bugging Amber as well.

"I don't know of anyone who does," Nora said gently.

Amber nodded, a small smile on her face as if she was grateful for Nora's understanding.

"I asked Raul if he would be willing to sign one," Amber said as she tucked an errant curl behind her ear.

Nora felt her eyes go wide. This was an unexpected turn of events. Amber had been adamant she didn't even want to mention the document to her fiancé.

"Why?" Nora asked before she could think through her question.

"My family kept asking about it. I just . . . I'm not sure why I asked, really. We were in the middle of a conversation about his family and when I would get to meet them and it felt like he was evading me. I know he wants to take me when he can afford it but right now so much of his income goes back to his family that it's hard for him to imagine saving up for a trip like that. I told him maybe to put his pride aside for a second and let me pay travel costs so the people he loves most in the world can meet. And he said—" Amber held her arms around her middle as she continued. "He wasn't sure when I could meet his family."

She bit her lip as if trying to control herself before speaking once more. "I thought that was odd. I mean, why? Wouldn't you be dying to introduce the love of your life to your family? I felt like he had been and then during that conversation everything had changed. He tried to backtrack and said he wasn't sure his family was ready to meet me yet. That they were still pretty worried about him getting married so fast, something I swore he'd never said before but he insisted he had. And then I just asked him. What would he think about signing a prenup?"

Nora held her breath as she waited for Amber to answer. She knew the answer couldn't have been good, considering the conversation they were having. Even as she was sure Raul wasn't who he said he was, she still held onto a small hope that she was all wrong. For Amber's sake she wished it over and over again. But this conversation was only solidifying Nora's concerns about Raul.

"He laughed, thinking it was a joke. To be fair, I'd told him I'd never consider one so I could see why he thought it was a joke. But then I told him I was serious and his demeanor did a one-eighty like I've never seen. He wasn't just serious; he became furious. Yelling about me changing my mind on him. I told him I was just thinking about it and wondered what he thought. And he said, 'You know what I think? I think this is complete BS. And you can take your question and shove it. I will never, ever sign a prenup.' Then he stormed out of the room."

Amber wrung her hands, her eyes on them as if afraid to look at her mother.

Nora stood and quickly made her way to her daughter before enveloping her in a hug.

"When did this happen?" she asked softly as she rubbed Amber's back.

"Two days ago," Amber whispered against Nora's shoulder.

For two days her baby girl had been holding onto this?

Nora closed her eyes and hugged even tighter.

"I apologized. Told Raul it wasn't fair of me to bring the prenup up in the way that I had. I was sure after I apologized he'd realize how he'd overreacted and tell me that he'd thought about it and we should at least have a conversation about it but instead he just said 'good.' As if the matter was over. He'd yelled at me and that was it. His word was law."

Amber shook her head as dampness seeped into Nora's shirt from Amber's tears. Nora felt her own threatening to fall.

Nora's relationship with Amber's dad had been a lot like the one Amber was describing and she wouldn't wish that kind of abuse on anyone. Granted, Amber's dad had been a teen on drugs so Nora could kind of understand his behavior. Raul, on the other hand, was a grown man in his right mind. What was his excuse for lashing out at Amber and scaring her like this?

Nora could feel Amber trembling against her.

This was about so much more than a prenup. But was Amber ready to hear it?

Nora wanted desperately to save her daughter but she couldn't be saved unless she chose to. That was one of the hardest things about terrible relationships.

"I'm here," Nora assured before saying anything else. Amber needed to know that Nora was always in her corner.

"I had always felt like the idea of not signing a prenup was all me. But looking back, I see the way Raul twisted our conversations, made things seem like my ideas. What I thought were my thoughts were really his. I reflected his wishes because I wanted so desperately to please him. I love him so much." Amber's voice broke at the same moment as Nora's heart. How she wished she could do more. But right now Amber needed a listening ear. The rest could come later.

"Do you think there could be other things in our relationship that are like this? And if so, what is our relationship based on?"

Nora could see that Amber was slowly coming to terms with things but she couldn't quite see what the rest of them could. And Nora couldn't force it. Everything about Amber's position was tentative.

"The more I've been thinking, the more I realized that I've been unfair when it came to the prenup. I was so intent on protecting my relationship that I didn't even think about what not signing one would do to Elise. The position it would leave her in. And you." Amber pulled away to look into Nora's eyes. "You invested so much into this place. If Raul decides to leave me and claims half of the inn, where does that leave all of us?"

Nora didn't think that would happen even in the worst-case scenario, but Amber was right. Not signing a prenup left all of them exposed. Something they were willing to do for Amber. Not so much for Raul.

Nora also noticed the way Amber had said 'if Raul leaves me.' Not 'if one of us leaves.' She was all in. But she was starting to doubt that Raul was.

Her poor girl. But even as Nora ached, she had to stay strong.

"What do you want to do?" Nora asked, letting Amber take the lead even though it physically pained her to restrain her own opinion. She wanted to march up to Raul and tell him just what she thought of him. To order him to pack up his behind and get off the island for good. That no man would ever talk to her daughter in such a way and stay in their lives. That Amber was much too incredible for him, and he was an idiot not to see what was right in front of him. But this wasn't up to Nora.

"I think I need him to sign a prenup if we're going to get married," Amber finally said in a raspy whisper, leaning heavily against the door now that she was no longer hugging Nora.

Amber was bone tired; the bags under her eyes were hard to miss. Nora was going to guess that Amber had barely slept since her fight with Raul two days before.

"I owe you and Elise that much," Amber added.

Don't do it for us was on the tip of Nora's tongue. But even as she wanted Amber to do this for herself, Nora wasn't sure Amber quite had that strength. Many didn't. But Amber could stand up for those she loved even when she couldn't do it for herself. Nora had to let Amber do this in her way. For them, and in the end it would be for her as well.

Because Nora was almost positive how her conversation with Raul would go.

And as thrilled as she was that Amber would finally see Raul for the man he was, she was already hurting just imagining the pain it would cause for dear, sweet Amber. Breakups, no matter how necessary, were never cut and dried. Too much emotion lay in the aftermath for it to be anything but messy.

"I'd appreciate it if you let us know when you decide to talk to him. I'd rather you not be alone for that conversation," Nora tried to say in the most diplomatic way. If Raul had blown up at the mere mention of a prenup, Nora wasn't sure what the man would do if Amber pressed. She didn't want to find out.

"He won't hurt me, Mama Nora," Amber said even as she gripped the doorknob behind her so hard that her knuckles went white.

"Please?" was all Nora could say. She wasn't going to argue with Amber. She wasn't going to tell her that she couldn't be sure of anything. Nora knew how love could make you feel sure of those kinds of things, confident that being hurt by that person was utterly impossible. And even after you had been hurt, trying to find what you must have done wrong because surely the other person wouldn't have done what they had without good reason.

Amber locked eyes with Nora, and Nora swore there were at least a hundred thoughts that tore through Amber's mind. Amber finally nodded before turning and leaving the room.

Nora wanted to chase after her, to make sure she was okay, but she could tell Amber needed time to herself and those hundreds of thoughts.

So with a heavy heart Nora turned back to her painting. What else could she do? But as she raised her brush she could already feel she was in a bad headspace. And painting in a bad space was never a good idea.

She placed her brush in an empty cup and gazed out the window. The typically gray weather that hung over Whisling in the fall was out in full effect that day. The clouds were low and heavy, promising rain, and yet there was still an indescribable beauty about the place. One that Nora had come to adore.

But today she needed the sunshine. She needed bright and

happy. She needed something more. And she knew exactly where to get it.

THE GALLERY WAS quiet when Nora walked in. She'd guessed it would be, considering it wasn't peak visitor season. Although word of Deb's gallery had gotten around and even when Whisling wasn't experiencing much tourist activity, interested visitors often came just for the art that Deb curated.

And probably to see Mack's handsome face. Nora knew for a fact that many women came in who would only buy art from Mack.

Nora grinned, knowing others in her place might have been jealous. But to love Mack meant dealing with adoring women. And having the confidence in their relationship and herself to believe that Mack would never reciprocate the overtly flirtatious gestures. Sure, that might place Nora in the exact same spot Amber was in, trusting that her partner would never hurt her, but Nora knew that with Mack things were different. And although she couldn't really be sure of anything, she had to trust Mack. Or their relationship would be over.

"To what do I owe the pleasure of Whisling Island's most talented artist gracing our humble gallery?" Mack asked as he walked around the counter to greet Nora. He took her into his arms and gave her a kiss that he probably shouldn't have, considering they were in front of glass windows that showed them off to all who were traversing this part of Elliot Drive.

Nora pulled away before she was ready, but they really shouldn't be giving any potential customers quite this show.

"I needed a ray of sunshine," Nora said honestly as Mack still held her close.

"Is that all I am to you?" Mack asked with mock hurt. "Your little ray of sunshine?"

"Would it be so bad?" Nora teased back.

Mack chuckled. "No, it wouldn't be. Not at all."

Nora smiled and just as she'd hoped, her mood lifted. She still felt horribly for Amber and her stomach turned at just the thought of what was in their near future, but it didn't seem so bleak.

"Quiet day?" Nora asked, looking around. She knew she should step out of Mack's embrace. It wasn't professional in the least, but considering her sister owned the place, Nora figured she should be allowed a few liberties. She didn't think Deb would mind this at all.

"It's been pretty busy, believe it or not. You just caught me at the right time," Mack said as he looked toward the door.

"Are you here alone?" Nora asked. Typically they worked in pairs at the gallery. First, it ensured there was always a gallery representative for customers to speak to, even if one was busy, and second, for safety reasons. The gallery was known to hold some nearly priceless pieces. In fact, Deb was looking into hiring a full-time security guard because the gallery was beginning to attract more and more prestigious artists and their work.

"Deb and Luke are in back unpacking Beaufoy's latest collection." Mack let go of Nora just long enough to point to the door that led to the back room of the gallery.

Nora couldn't help but grin at the name Mack had said. Beaufoy had been one of Deb's early finds. The artist had emigrated from France to the Pacific Northwest to pursue his love of the unique landscape here. When Deb had begun her gallery, Beaufoy was one of the first artists she'd showcased. The man was now quite popular, even a household name in the art crowds, but he still insisted on only showing his work in Deb's gallery. The man was as loyal as they came.

"I'm sure you'll sell them all before my next shift," Nora said as she nudged Mack with her hip.

"Considering you work about once a month these days, I'd better," Mack replied.

Nora laughed. Her work schedule wasn't quite as sporadic as Mack indicated but it was close. If her boss had been anyone other than her sister she would surely have been fired for her frequent inability to work. Thankfully Deb was not only a gracious boss but a supportive sister and had encouraged Nora to take her time with the paintings for Genevieve's wedding rather than work her shifts at the gallery.

Nora was about to make her light retort when her phone chimed.

Her heart dropped. She wasn't sure how she knew who it was, but she did.

Sure enough, the text read, *He's on lunch break. I can't wait any longer. I'll be talking to him at my place.*

"I have to get back to the inn," Nora said, her words falling over each other in her panic.

"Is everything okay?" Mack asked, still holding Nora. His arms were tight around her waist, letting her know he wasn't going anywhere.

Nora just shook her head. She'd had a bad feeling about Amber's future conversation with Raul and now that feeling was churning powerfully in her belly. Why had she been so selfish that she'd left for her ray of sunshine instead of staying for when Amber would need her? Granted, she'd had no clue Amber would act so soon, but . . .

Nora pushed off of Mack's chest. She had to get out of there.

"Deb!" Mack called out, causing his boss to come running out of the back.

"Nora?" Deb asked with a puzzled frown. She'd probably expected an intruder or worse from Mack's loud call for help.

"She has to go. She needs me," Mack managed to explain even though he had no idea what was going on.

Deb nodded. "Of course. We have it here. Call me when you can," she ordered either Nora or Mack; Nora wasn't sure. And she would call her sister after this had all played out, but right now she had to get to Amber.

Nora started a harried walk toward the door, almost stumbling.

Mack took her arm. Nora tried to shrug him off but he held firm. "You won't be getting anywhere if you trip and fall and hurt yourself," Mack insisted.

Nora knew he was right but pressed forward at the same pace, just with a little more stability, thanks to Mack.

"Thanks, Deb," Mack called over his shoulder as they left the gallery.

Mack led Nora to the passenger's seat of her car—thankfully she had a front row parking space—and then ran around to the driver's side as Nora put her keys into the ignition, still reprimanding herself.

If she got there too late . . . she couldn't think like that.

"What's going on?" Mack asked after he got on the road. The inn was a good ten minutes away even if Mack pushed the speed limit. They had more than enough time for Nora to explain the situation. Come to think of it, maybe it was a good thing Mack was here. If Raul did become physical . . . Nora rolled down the window even though it couldn't have been more than forty degrees outside. But her heaving stomach needed the fresh air.

Nora explained what Amber had told her and then what she had planned.

"You're afraid he might physically hurt her?" Mack asked.

Nora nodded. "He's proven he's not above bullying her into getting his way. If his loud words no longer work . . ."

Nora didn't want to finish that thought.

"Text Elise," Mack said.

Of course. Why hadn't Nora thought of that? Elise was on inn property and would be ready to protect Amber in whatever way she needed. She'd call the police or whatever was necessary to keep Amber safe. Things Amber wouldn't necessarily do for herself.

Nora's fingers shook as she typed out the text. She pressed send just as Mack turned up the drive to the inn. Nora wished she'd thought of texting Elise earlier. Now they might even beat Elise to their cottage, but the more people on hand to help Amber, the better.

Mack parked right in front of the cute home Amber shared with her sister and Nora threw her door open before the car came to a complete stop.

She tore over the rocky drive and ran up the few steps of the porch, coming to a sudden halt when sobbing greeted her ears.

If Raul had placed a finger on Amber, there would be hell to pay.

But as Nora threw the door open, Elise just steps behind her and Mack on Elise's heels, the only person Nora saw was Amber.

The poor woman was curled up in the fetal position on her couch, her hair in disarray and her hands over her face as cries of anguish tore through the air.

The sound was enough to bring Nora to her knees but she kept going until she fell to said knees beside the couch.

Nora had no idea what to do or say. She'd been prepared to fight Amber's foes but this wasn't a sight she'd been anticipating.

Nora put her arms around her sweet little girl and held her tight. What else could she do? She held her as she sobbed, Nora and Elise quickly joining in the tears even as they weren't quite sure what they were crying about. All they knew was that Amber had been hurt beyond compare and they were in deep pain with her.

Nora didn't know how much time had passed. It could have been just minutes or maybe much longer. She knew her eyes were gritty and her throat was sore and parched but beyond that she wasn't sure of much.

Gradually Amber's cries became a little softer, the wracking of her body a little less frequent as her sobs lessened.

"He's gone," Amber whispered hollowly.

It was all she could manage before another sob overwhelmed her.

Nora knew one day she'd say this was all for the best and mean it. But in that moment, feeling her daughter's acute pain, her own heart tearing to shreds, Nora knew she couldn't say it today. Because nothing felt right when someone you loved was breaking. So Nora would hold Amber, love her, and one day they would be okay. But today wasn't that day.

CHAPTER SIXTEEN

"SURPRISE!" The shouts reverberated from all around Julia as she put a hand to her chest. A few more birthdays and she wasn't sure how her heart would have reacted.

"What?" she asked, her blue eyes wide. She tried to take in the scene before her but it was too much.

She'd been expecting a quiet dinner with her dear friends Bess and Dax. Ellis had told her he wouldn't be able to make it home for her birthday, as tour prep was really ramping up. And Wendy had said she was going home to Travers that weekend.

Julia had understood. It was her fifty-fifth birthday. She'd had fifty-four before and God willing she'd have many more to come. There were more important things than celebrating the day.

But judging by the room full of people before her, people had wanted to celebrate her, even when she hadn't.

Julia felt tears prick at her eyes. She was not going to cry. Not today.

But then a man stepped out from behind the crowd, the man Julia had been craving since the moment he left the island.

"Ellis," she breathed as those tricky tears began to fall. There was no helping it.

He wrapped her in his arms and Julia breathed in the essence of Ellis. His fresh soap that he still insisted on using even though it was less than a dollar a bar, his minty breath, the smell of wood and brand new rain . . . Ellis was home.

He was here. Holding her. On her birthday.

"Why?" was all Julia managed through her tears.

The crowd laughed and began to mingle, giving the couple a quiet moment to themselves before the party started in full swing.

"Do you really think I'd miss my girl's birthday?" Ellis said. Julia loved how he insisted on calling her his girl even though her girlhood was far behind her. Ellis made Julia feel young and free as well as a timeless treasure—all at the same time.

"Considering that's exactly what you told me, yeah," Julia said as she held onto him even more tightly. How was she going to ever let go?

She wouldn't.

The thought came unbidden to her mind but when it did, she realized her truth. One she'd tell Ellis soon. Maybe as a gift to him on her birthday.

She'd started toying with the idea when her family was there, and had quickly realized she'd been silly to think that going with Ellis on tour would look like she was following him because she had nothing better to do. If the situation were reversed Ellis would one hundred percent move to anywhere Julia was shooting. And who cared what others thought of her, anyway?

And her other reason for staying? Wendy was fully independent. Not only did she have her own group of friends, but she had a boyfriend who was pretty dang fantastic. Even when Wendy couldn't take care of herself, they'd be there for her.

Ultimately, no one on the island needed Julia. And while she loved Whisling, she could leave for the length of a tour.

The only thing she needed, the only person she needed, was on tour. And she was pretty sure he needed her as well. So why was she staying home when she could be with him?

"Happy Birthday!" Nora exclaimed as she burst through the door, a giant smile on her face. Her outburst caused Julia to pull away from Ellis but only slightly. She stayed right beside him and he kept an arm around her waist. "I was worried I would ruin the surprise so I hid out in my car until I saw you all pass."

"I didn't see you," Julia assured her. Not that she'd been looking around at the cars parked near Bess's home, but she figured she would have noticed a person in a car.

"I ducked down the moment I heard any car. I peeked up over my dash just in time to see you turn into Bess's driveway," Nora explained and Julia laughed.

She loved that her friends were willing to go to such lengths to keep her surprise.

"How's Amber?" Julia asked immediately. The news hadn't spread far yet, but soon the entire island would know that Amber's fiancé had moved . . . without her. Julia wasn't sure of the specifics but she could imagine the poor girl was devastated.

"Distraught. But she'll make it," Nora said with a sigh. "In fact, I should probably get going soon. I try to stop by after she's done with work at the inn to make sure that she eats. She's tending to forget those basic life functions."

Julia nodded. She'd lived those post-heartbreak weeks before. Life didn't feel like it would go on. Until it did.

"She'll make it and so will you," Julia assured Nora because she could only imagine the kind of pain a mother felt over her child's heartbreak.

"Oh, I know I will. I'm in the would-it-really-be-so-bad-if-I-kill-Raul state right now."

Julia chuckled. She knew her friend was joking. Or at least she was pretty sure.

"But at least he had the decency to leave the island. Probably to try his scheme on some other unsuspecting woman. I wish I could have sent him off with a warning sign on his back and a kick to his pants."

Julia nodded. She would have wanted the same.

"And I know she'll make it too. It's just so hard. But I know she's better off. I can't imagine if she'd married him and then saw his true colors."

Julia nodded again, putting her arms around her stomach, Ellis holding her closer.

"Well, tell her I said hi if the time seems right."

This time Nora nodded.

"Oh!" Julia remembered a message she had for Nora's family. "And I have a certain former costar who keeps bugging me for info on a certain relative of yours."

"Aiden?" Nora asked, a gleam in her eyes.

Julia nodded.

"I knew it! He totally has it bad for Elise, right?" Nora asked.

"I'd say," Julia replied. "The man has never been known to pursue a woman like this before. Your Elise must have made quite the impression on him."

"You mean when she ignored or offended him?" Nora said with a smirk.

"She didn't," Julia replied but then again she could totally see the sassy and cute Elise doing just that. "I'm imagining that's not a reaction Aiden Christensen often receives."

"You could say that again," Nora agreed.

"So what should I tell him?" Julia asked.

"That gaining her affection and attention will be the hardest thing he's ever done. But she is more than worth it," Nora replied.

Julia grinned. She couldn't wait to relay that message. "I'm sure he'll find a reason to visit again before Genevieve's wedding. He was pretty upset when he had to leave the day after her wedding shower for a shoot."

"Wait, I've been meaning to ask you, why weren't you at the shower?" Nora raised an eyebrow as she waited for an answer.

Julia had been invited but had quickly turned down the invite. Her family had still been in town and the last thing she wanted was to bring her mom and sister to an event like Genevieve's. At best they would have insulted the bride-to-be, and at worst Genevieve would have offended them. Julia didn't see another outcome so she'd stayed away. Thankfully when she'd told Genevieve she had family obligations, Gen had understood.

"Lacey and Betty were in town," Julia explained.

"Ah, say no more." Nora waved a hand. She'd met the two when they'd all bumped into one another in town and Nora had later called Julia's relatives unique. That had been the right term, considering the way they'd treated Nora.

Although Julia's relationship with her family was improving, that didn't make them any more palatable for other people. Especially people her sister and mom were for some reason intent on offending, which meant every resident of anywhere other than Travers.

"Julia," Bess sing-songed and Julia turned to the rest of the party. She really had been neglecting them.

Not only were Bess and Dax there, but so were Deb and Luke, Gen and Levi, Olivia and Dean, Lily and Allen, Piper and Carter, and Alexis and Jared, as well as Lou.

Julia made a quick scan of the room, hoping the last woman would have brought her guy that Julia had heard a bit about.

She didn't know much, but she heard furtive whisperings of a certain guitar teacher who had his eye fixed on their beautiful Lou. But because he wouldn't date his students, he and Lou hadn't had a chance to explore anything more than friendship even though he was present at all of Cash's soccer games. Even though she was disappointed not to meet him, Julia was just grateful that Lou seemed one hundred percent over her lout of an ex.

"I'd better go. But have a great birthday," Nora said as she squeezed Julia's arm and gave her an air kiss.

Julia waved after her friend and then turned back to her other friends. They'd all shown up for her.

Julia gave Bess a giant hug. "How did you keep this a secret?" she demanded.

"Because all I had to do was show up. Your darling boyfriend took care of the rest," Bess said as she patted Ellis on the back. Although he'd had to let go of Julia so that she could hug Bess, he was still close at her side, as though making up for their time apart by keeping as physically close as he could tonight.

Julia kissed Ellis's cheek.

"Thank you all for coming," Julia said, unsure of how to respond. The gesture was so great, a simple thank you seemed insufficient.

"We all love you, Juls!" Deb exclaimed and Julia could more than feel that love.

She went around giving hugs to all of her guests, saving Ellis for last. His hug was the longest and best, as it should be.

Julia stood with Ellis in quiet comfort as she listened to the conversations around her. Lily and Gen were at the appetizer table, filling plates and sharing a laugh about the antics of their young daughters. Deb and Bess were comparing their kids' college bills, Deb lamenting that her kids thought she was made of cash now that the gallery was thriving. Piper and Carter seemed in their own little world. Julia didn't blame them. A little bird had told her about their elopement. No one had been the least bit surprised that the two had found their way back to one another or that they'd eloped. It was so like them. Julia was just grateful they had taken time out of their love-induced bliss to come to her party.

"Happy Birthday," Lou said loudly as she, Alexis, and Jared joined Julia and Ellis.

"Thank you," Julia said genuinely as Ellis smiled to greet their friends. He knew this was the core group caring for Julia while he was gone and was never shy about expressing his gratitude for them. "I have to admit when I saw you here I was hoping you were hiding your guitar teacher somewhere," Julia teased.

She loved the redness that tinted Lou's cheeks. The woman really was smitten. Too bad it had to be so complicated. But Lou was no stranger to complications. She'd experienced them in her own marriage as well as in her divorce. And so had her best friend and stepsister Alexis, although it seemed like Alexis's trials weren't nearly as large as they had been.

"He's not *my* guitar teacher," Lou said but then amended, "well, he is my guitar teacher, and that's a big part of the problem."

The group laughed.

"This conversation is going in a direction I'm not sure I want to be a part of. I'm going to grab some food," Lou said with a grin.

The others laughed but Lou made good on her threat, joining Lily and Gen at the food table.

"I'm gonna get something too. I haven't eaten since I got to the island and I'm starved. Want something, Sweetheart?" Ellis asked.

Julia wasn't sure what the offerings were but she was hungry as well since she'd come expecting one of Bess' incredible dinners. "Just grab a little of everything," she instructed.

Ellis grinned and turned to do what she'd asked. The man was a treasure.

"I've heard good things about your household," Julia said to Alexis and Jared.

"Do you mean the part where my young daughter was dating a boy way older than her?"

Julia's eyes went wide. She hadn't heard about that.

"Oh, I'm guessing that's news to you. I was sure the entire island knew, considering how many moms came into my office trying to tell me how I should parent Brittany," Jared said when he saw Julia's reaction.

"I'm sorry," Julia said. She couldn't imagine that had been fun.

"Don't be. I always knew raising a daughter was going to be my greatest pleasure and the thing that took me to the brink of death," Jared joked with a grin.

Julia laughed.

"But good news: she doesn't hate me anymore," Alexis said, raising her arms in the air.

"Yeah, now she just hates me," Jared replied.

Julia continued laughing. She always felt a little ache at never raising children of her own. But then she'd hear things like this and think wow, she'd really dodged a bullet.

"But it's worth it. Our somewhat functional but highly irregular family can now move forward in the way we all want it to," Jared said, his gaze going to his girlfriend and seeming to promise so much to come.

Julia was thrilled for Alexis. She knew that Jared would have probably still found a way to be with Alexis even if Brittany continued to disapprove. But the road would have not been nearly as pleasant as it was now going to be. Although Julia foresaw speedbumps she also predicted many beautiful moments.

"Here you go." Ellis offered a plate to Julia. In his other hand he held another that was piled just as high.

"Oh, that looks amazing. Should we?" Alexis asked Jared.

The two headed toward the food bar, leaving Julia and Ellis alone.

Now was the time. Who knew when they'd have another minute alone? And Julia wanted to announce to her friends tonight that she was leaving.

She'd miss them, but not nearly as much as she'd missed Ellis.

"So I was thinking," Julia began as she popped a stuffed mushroom into her mouth and moaned, temporarily distracted. She'd missed out on three decades of eating good food. She was now making up for lost time.

"Good thinking or bad thinking?" Ellis asked as he followed her example. He too seemed to appreciate the savory flavors, if his grin indicated anything.

"I hope good," Julia said, setting down her plate on a table behind one of Bess's couches.

"Okay," Ellis said, his attention on Julia, but he continued eating. Julia didn't blame him.

"Is your offer still good?" Julia asked, suddenly feeling shy. She clasped her hands in front of her as she waited for Ellis to answer.

"What offer?" Ellis asked with a raised eyebrow as he too set down his plate. He seemed to anticipate what was coming.

"Can I still go on tour with you?" Julia asked. She pressed her lips together anxiously as she waited for his response.

"Seriously?" Ellis asked. "Because this wouldn't be a funny joke."

"Seriously," she affirmed.

Ellis yelped and lifted her into the air, swinging her in a circle. Julia pulled her feet close to keep from kicking anything but laughed at his antics.

"What's going on?" Dax asked. Ellis' enthusiasm had been impossible for the other partygoers to miss.

"My Julia is going on tour with me," Ellis announced proudly.

Cheers sounded from around the room and Julia realized this was what she should have done all along. She was meant to be by Ellis' side.

As the cheers died down and conversations picked up once more, Ellis turned to Julia.

"Why?" he asked.

Julia smiled. "Because I miss you. And as much as I love Whisling it doesn't feel like home without you. You are now my home."

Ellis grinned even wider. "You're my home too, Julia."

He then told Julia with a kiss just how much he appreciated her decision, not caring a bit about the whoops and hollers that accompanied that kiss.

Julia didn't either. Because she felt in her core that she'd made the right decision. Being away from Ellis had felt like one long night, waiting for the light to come. Now that he was here, she couldn't let him go. The night was over, and it was time to enjoy the sunshine. Her sunshine. Her home.

JULIA CLEMENS

Julia Clemens always dreamed of putting stories to paper and now she gets to live that dream with her two adorable boys and one handsome hubby. From the sandy shores of Maui to the Rocky Mountains and then back to another island in the Pacific, serene Japan, Julia has lived around the world and found that even though all of these places are majestic with their natural beauty, the thing that makes every place so special...are the people. So she writes about those people and loves every minute of it.

Julia loves to hear from her readers so please reach out to her @ AuthorJuliaClemens@yandex.com